MY LIFE on FiRE

nosy crow

To all the good friends out there

C. H.

First published in the UK in 2023 by Nosy Crow Ltd
Wheat Wharf, 27a Shad Thames,
London, SE1 2XZ, UK

Nosy Crow Eireann Ltd
44 Orchard Grove, Kenmare,
Co Kerry, V93 FY22, Ireland

ISBN: 978 1 83994 283 9

A CIP catalogue record for this book will be available from the British Library.

Printed and bound in Great Britain by Clays Ltd, Elcograf S.p.A.
Typeset by Tiger Media.

Papers used by Nosy Crow are made from wood grown in sustainable forests.

1 3 5 7 9 10 8 6 4 2

www.nosycrow.com

Chapter 1
Ren

Houses don't burn down. That's wrong.

"I'll huff and I'll puff and I'll blow your house down," says the wolf in the story for little kids.

The truth is, houses burn *up*.

We saw the flames when we were sitting inside our car at the end of our road … leaping orange tongues of fire bigger than a firework display and crowds of people and fire engines.

We thought it was exciting.

But then, as we drove nearer, we all whispered, "*That's our house!*"

When we climbed out of the car, there was a

big cheer from our neighbours because they had thought we were trapped inside. Everyone rushed over and hugged us. We didn't die or anything. I wouldn't be telling this if we'd died.

No one knows for certain how the fire began that Sunday evening. Mum and Dad said it might be faulty electrics, but we might never know for sure. We had spent the evening at Mum's friend Lisa's house: me, Mum, Dad and my brother Petie. There we were, tucked up on the sofa eating pizza and watching films, and all that time my bedroom at home must have been flickering with orange light. That's how I picture it: flickering as the fire took hold.

By the time we drove back home and found the crowds and fire engines, our house must have been burning for at least two hours, one of the firemen said. The downstairs study had exploded with a bang everyone had heard down the street. That's when the people next door called the fire brigade. The Eltons stood in their coats, holding each other. Water was being sprayed on their bungalow too but it was just our house that was blazing because there was a garage in between our two houses.

Mum and Dad were pushed back. We all were.

We stood there gaping.

A fireman called, "Sorry, no one can go past the tape. Stay back until the area has been made safe!"

More firemen held on to hoses and huge jets of water spurted out into the building. Blue lights flashed, making it almost like day.

"We're so lucky," Mum said, holding me close. "Thank God we weren't inside."

"So lucky!" Dad echoed, holding Petie. "We're all OK. That's all that matters."

There was a feeling of rushing and shouts but somehow I was closed off, frozen, watching. My eyes had fixed themselves on our burning home. Those blooms of sudden light as things inside caught fire and blazed. Those burning bits that flew and fizzled. *Swishing* … *whishing* … Black smoke billowing out from downstairs. *Hiss, spit, crack,* making me gasp.

Worst of all, our house was already broken. I was looking up into my own bedroom but chopped in half as if someone had sliced it with a giant knife. I could see my bed and chest of drawers, my stool and fallen-over lamp. There were my kite curtains blowing, my otter picture tipping all wonky on the wall.

I turned and pushed my face into Dad's chest to not see. But I had seen.

We watched the fire devour our house like a monster.

Houses don't burn down. They burn up and up into the sky with huge flames that eat everything until there's nothing left.

Chapter 2

Ren

A woman in a dressing gown opened her front door. She bit her lip. "Two kiddies. It'll be a bit of a squish, I'm afraid, but it's all that's left."

"Thank you," Mum and Dad both said.

She pointed and we all followed her up the stairs. "There's two doubles," she said. "No noise after ten p.m. Shared bathroom. No cooking in the rooms. No guests. No clothes washing – take it to a launderette."

The bed blocked the door. Petie and me squeezed through and clambered on to it. Mum and Dad squashed in behind us. The windowpane looked milky; you couldn't see out properly. Once you'd sat on the bed there wasn't anywhere else to go. There was a wardrobe with a door hanging open. Inside it was just a brown nothing. Dad skirted round the bed and pushed the wardrobe door shut. It made a crunching noise and fell open again.

I couldn't think properly. Petie and me sat on the bed holding carrier bags.

Mum and Dad said, "Stay there," and disappeared out into the corridor. We could hear them whispering. *We had to go somewhere… Not even clean.*

"It smells in here," Petie said.

He was right; it smelled of old things and smoke. But then I realised the smoky smell was coming from us: our clothes and hair. We were smoke people. Petie had a smudgy mark on his cheek. When I looked down, my trainers were spattered with black dust.

Petie nudged me. "Will there be breakfast, Ren?"

"I don't know." I felt lost, as if I'd wandered away from life. All that noise and the fire and the rushing people … and now just this gloomy room with a dim lamp flickering over our heads.

Petie swung his legs. "Will we have bacon and

eggs, Ren?"

"I said I don't know."

"If we were on a holiday, there would be a special breakfast."

By my side of the bed, the carpet had a dark stain.

"Waffles?"

I ignored him, staring at the stain.

Petie scrambled over and stared at it too. "Did the carpet get burned?"

I shrugged. I sat back on the bed. The wallpaper had a brown splodgy pattern. A dark-blue mark on the bottom of the wall looked like a speckled bruise. At home my bedroom walls had fluffy clouds shaped like the backs of sheep with a rainbow behind each one. When she came to say goodnight, Mum sometimes said to me, "Which cloud are you hiding in?" and I always said, "That one over there," choosing one. I loved my wallpaper. Mum and Dad always said I had my head in the clouds. I liked taking my mind somewhere else. Floating away. "You're a dreamer, Ren," they would say.

That's why I loved my collections inside my little painted cupboard with the glass doors. They were perfect for dreaming. All the shelves were crammed with hand-picked animals, souvenirs and birthday presents. There were painted ornaments, shells, glass animals and birds. I liked to move them about and put different ones at the front. "How is the art exhibition?" Dad would say. When I was younger than Petie, I used to imagine my animal collections having their own life, calling to each other, "Quick, she's coming!" and dashing back into their places a split second before I checked them. Now, sitting in the smelly room, I felt waves of sadness crash over me. Our home. My bedroom and all those special things… Where were my collections now? A horrible twisting feeling gripped me inside and I started crying.

Petie nudged me again. "Will we stay up late?"

"I don't know. It's already late. Leave me alone."

"But will we?"

"I don't care about staying up!"

The door opened and Mum and Dad appeared. Mum pointed to my carrier bag. Mrs Collis had handed it to Mum while the firemen were rolling up the hoses. "For tonight," she said. "We'll get you some proper things tomorrow, love." The clothes in the bag were from Alice Collis, her daughter. She was thirteen. I dug around. Alice's pants. Pyjamas.

A blue jumper and a knitted hat.

My only clothes.

Dad must have seen I was crying. "Shush now," he said. He hugged me to him. "Come on, love. Tell you what, put your pyjamas on, then you can settle down."

Mum and Dad talked again quietly by the door. "It's very, very late. Dad and I are going to be just in the room next door," Mum said.

But Petie leapt up and stretched his arms out. "Cuddle!" he shouted.

"It's bedtime," Mum said.

"Cuddle!" he howled. He jumped into Mum's arms, sobbing.

"Shush," said Mum. She and Dad looked at each other.

The landlady's voice called up from downstairs, sharp and clear. "Try to be quiet, please. Some people are already asleep."

Mum sighed and said to Dad, "I'll have Petie. You sleep in here with Ren." She patted my head and kissed me. "Night-night." Then the door closed.

Dad stared out of the window. A long sigh came from him that was a groan too. He turned back to me and took the pyjamas out of the carrier bag.

"Come on, love, bedtime."

I got ready for bed. My movements seemed strange and slow. Dad stared out of the window, even though it was so dark you couldn't see a thing.

I put Alice's jumper on over the pyjamas. It was down to my knees but it made me warm. The sheets were scratchy.

Dad piled the coats on the floor so I could get in bed. He sat beside me and pushed his hair out of his eyes. "Try to sleep. I know you've got a lot of questions, Ren, love. We all have. We've had a big shock. Things will look better in the morning."

I kept noticing the weird smell. It was in my nose: sour roses mixed with smoky petrol.

Try to sleep.

The second I closed my eyes, flames jumped in front of them. My little animals, all my precious things, were flying out of my cupboard, like birds. I clutched and grabbed as they disappeared in smoke. The more I clutched handfuls to me, the more they kept dropping out and away and down into swirling dark.

My eyes jerked open. My breath came in little bursts.

I rolled over. Next to me, Dad lay curled up.

His breathing was a big sound in the room, low and rumbly. In the dim light I realised he was still wearing his shirt from today. He should have had Alice's pyjamas – they would have fitted him better than me.

I lay there and listened to his loud breathing. It helped. My eyes closed again.

✗

Next thing I knew I was waking up and it was morning.

But Dad was wrong when he said everything would look better. Everything looked just as horrible as it had last night.

Our house had gone.

We had fallen off the edge of the world.

Chapter 3
Caspar

My name is Caspar.

I've decided to begin by explaining about our teacher.

She arrived at the start of this autumn term.

She was called Miss Chatto. I liked her name. It sounded friendly already. And she was.

My dad said, "That woman looks about twelve, far too young to be a teacher." But Miss Chatto was actually twenty-six. This was her first teaching job and we were her first class. I heard Mr Winkworth telling Miss Allen. Not the age bit; I worked out her age when Miss Chatto mentioned a song that had come out the year she was born. I looked it up when I got home.

Miss Chatto smiled a lot for a teacher and she had a little laugh that seemed to float up to the top of the classroom. There were four notes in it: haha, ha, haaa. "Welcome. I hope you will be really happy."

People started volunteering for things. We were all clamouring to be noticed by Miss Chatto.

She said, "Could a few of you come in sometimes and sort out the room ready for the afternoon?" and when lots of hands went up she laughed and said, "Goodness! That's amazing, guys." I liked that she called us *guys*. It sounded older and more like we were all part of a fun plan.

I wanted to know everything about Miss Chatto. I already knew her birthday and her car, the red Mini in the car park, two years old. I thought her favourite colour was probably purple because she wore purple jumpers.

I started helping at lunchtime. We piled up the literacy books and tidied the reading corner or sharpened pencils. Sometimes, when she was in the classroom, she called us *the team*. *"Hi, team!"* She wore rings on her thumb and a sparkly pink one on the middle finger of her right hand. Her fingers were long and elegant, like someone who played the piano. She laughed and we talked about all kinds of things like films and books and sandwich fillings. She preferred sushi for lunch. She brought it in a lunch box with a flowery lid. She made the sushi herself. I said I would like to try to make some and she said she would teach us. Her head did a little roll when she was pleased about something, like someone in warm sunshine enjoying a moment of it.

Things can happen suddenly. If you were a boat, you could be sailing along on a bright sunny day, waving at dolphins, and then, *woomph*, a storm could blow up and suddenly you could be fighting to stay on the sea, or even to stay alive. Life's strange.

When term began, our class were all making papier mâché balloons for our topic about world geography. You should try it. You take an actual balloon, inflate it and cover it with strips of newspaper soaked in glue. There need to be several layers and you have to leave your balloon to dry between layers before you can paint it. But the finished thing is amazing. You can add a basket to make a hot-air balloon.

Miss Chatto opened a packet and handed out balloons. "So, we've only got the correct number of balloons, everyone," she said. "You have to look after your balloon and not burst it." I think this was a wise move because lots of people think it's funny to burst balloons and this put us *on our guard*. We all wanted to get on to the decorating stage and if we popped our balloons we would never get there. I took extreme care with my balloon and was actually quite slow and Mr Charles, who helps in our class, said, "Caspar, speed up. The glued strips don't have to be perfect; they just have to cover all of it." If someone gives me an instruction, I try to follow it, but I also liked watching everyone else and that slowed me down.

We worked in pairs. My partner was Sohail. Teachers came round to encourage us. I got a lot of glue on my sleeves because they wriggled down and got soaked. I got a lot on my hands obviously. We were having a great time. We put our covered balloons on a table at the back. Next day, in the afternoon, we did another layer of gluing. Some people in my class would be quite happy to do papier mâché and gluing practically every day. We all got to chat and make a mess. It was pretty much perfect.

The plan was to hang our finished hot-air balloons all along the corridor before parents' evening. After the second day of working really hard, we were back outside the classrooms, early in the morning on day three, ready to start painting our finished balloons. Our classrooms face the playground on one side, with glass doors and a bench.

When we lined up, we saw that the door to our classroom was already wide open, even though the teachers were still coming out from the side door by the hall to collect us. All the parents had waved and gone away and we were standing chatting when … *crash!*

I looked inside the classroom and saw a sudden movement: a jagged black shape swishing across the window in a big diagonal.

The teachers crept to the door and paused on the step. They looked around and disappeared inside. It felt like a brave thing to do!

Our tidy line disintegrated, and we crowded round the window to peer in, getting really close in moments of bravery, then leaping back. No one followed the teachers inside.

"What's in there?" we asked each other.

Then there was a massive commotion with jagged shapes and beating sounds and things crashing. Miss Chatto burst out, calling, "Stay back, everyone! There's a bird in there."

A bird… My heart hammered. Poor bird! It must be completely panicking.

Lots of things happened then like Mr Collins the caretaker running round and disappearing inside, odd high cries and things hitting the window and a terrible feeling of disaster.

Miss Chatto came back out. Inside the classroom, the lights went off. Mr Charles came out too. They shushed us with fingers on their lips and made us stand further away.

I kept thinking of the bird and its wings hitting things. Every so often there would be a moment where you saw a flash of black as the bird crashed into the window. Somebody said it was a crow. They're nosy birds; we get them in my garden. If its wings were spread wide, they would take up so much air space.

This bit didn't actually last that long, maybe

five minutes, but it felt long because we were all shocked. The next thing we knew, the caretaker came out of our classroom carrying a box wrapped in an art overall. It was the kind of box the photocopying paper comes in. The bird must be inside. We stepped away, like miles away, to make sure we didn't get hit by feathers or something. Mr Collins carried the box across the playground and up on to the field. Then he put it down and stood back.

As we watched, movements began underneath the cloth: wriggling, poking and then, in a great burst, the crow took off and flew with the cloth wrapped round its leg for a few seconds, then the cloth fell off on to the grass. The bird soared up and up and was gone.

It was very exciting. We were thrilled. Until we got into our classroom and saw, well, devastation really. Broken balloons, equipment on the floor, paint bottles tipped and spilled, great slithery stains up the windows. Our classroom was a wreck.

We were taken to the small hall where we sat, dazed, while the adults cleaned. "Silent reading," they said. No one read. It wasn't silent.

When we were finally allowed back, a lot of things had been thrown away or put away and there was a strong smell of cleaning spray. Out on the tables, many people's balloons lay in bits.

Theo held up the crushed remains of his balloon. "I spent hours on this," he said, shaking his head. "It's totally ruined!"

Ellie was in tears. "Can I glue mine back together?"

Miss Chatto shook her head. "You'd be better off starting a new one. So sorry, honey."

It was like the massacre of the balloons. Our teachers kept trying to soothe everybody. My balloon was actually OK. I checked it carefully, pressing on the hard surface all over. It can't have been one of the ones the desperate bird had struck.

Miss Chatto said, "We need to have a chat about this. You all know no one is allowed inside school before the day starts and yet someone must have come inside for something and then left the glass door wide open. That person is in this room and knows who they are. Someone needs to own up. Did one of you come in to get a football? Or put away a coat?" She was doing that thing of staring at each person slowly, going right round the room.

"Why did the crow come inside anyway?" I asked.

"It may have thought there was food inside. We have no way of knowing. Please ... someone just own up. Which of you came inside before school and left the door wide open?"

"Can I ask a bit more about the bird?" I said.

"No, Caspar," Miss Chatto said. "We've already talked about it."

"It's just ... I'm wondering if it was injured?"

Her mouth went tight. "I'm not discussing it, Caspar."

Nobody else said anything. The room felt like a miserable place. Everyone looked at everyone else like after a murder on TV when the detective is waiting for someone to crack. There were so many ruined balloons, like precious broken eggshells after a giant had had a big breakfast.

Someone was going to have to own up and say they did it. You couldn't blame the crow. Someone must be feeling really terrible. This person would always be the balloon smasher. What a horrible feeling. And just for making a little mistake. At that moment it felt like all of us were bad. Once someone owned up, it would feel like everyone could breathe again. The feeling in the room was too horrible.

I stood up. "I'm owning up," I said.

The teachers looked at each other, frowning. There was a murmur of comments around the room.

"Do you mean it *was* you?" our teacher asked.

"Well ... it *could* have been," I said.

Miss Chatto sighed. "This has happened before, hasn't it, Caspar? This owning-up thing. It wasn't you who left the door wide open, was it?"

I sighed too. "OK then, no. I just wanted everyone to feel better. If I own up, at least nobody else will get blamed. And tomorrow I'm going to bring in buns. I'm going to make some at home, as soon as I get back."

Miss Chatto gazed at me. "Buns?"

"I want to help," I said.

She shook her head. "Caspar, you can't help."

"Oh," I said, "but they'll be good buns."

Her mouth turned to a flat line. "SIT DOWN, CASPAR."

It must be hard being a teacher.

When Dad collected me later in the day, Miss Chatto had a little chat with him and as we waited for the bus, he said, "Caspar, I know you meant well, but you can't own up to something you didn't do."

"Never?" I asked.

"No. You just have to be truthful."

"I just wanted everyone to feel better."

"That was kind of you but sometimes, when someone does something wrong, it's not your problem to fix."

All the time I was making the buns at home, I thought about the crow. It must have been truly scared to be inside our classroom. There was still a splodge high up where a wing must have crashed into the wall: a grey "V", almost like a flying bird. It looked a tiny bit bloody. I don't think anyone could reach high enough to clean off the mark. Birds can't figure out windows, Dad told me. Some birds crash into them when they're stressed or if the windows are very clean and they don't realise they're there. Dad said it's a good excuse for not cleaning your windows.

I got out all the ingredients and made enough buns for each person in my class and finished them with orange icing and a jelly sweet in the middle.

The next day my class were told that someone had owned up about the door, told their parents and said sorry to the teachers and now we were drawing a line under it. Our class still didn't know who was responsible. The person must have sat there and not given themselves away. There was lots of discussion about who that person might be, but it got a bit boring. So we all made our balloons again. Mine was solid and dry now so I painted it yellow.

I was allowed to give out my buns at break. You should do what you can to fix a bad thing. I couldn't help with the bird that crashed and hurt itself inside our classroom, but I could do something to make my class feel better.

Miss Chatto chose a bun and took it away with her to the staffroom to have with some tea. "I think you might be a one-off, Caspar," she told me, frowning and smiling and frowning again.

I liked Miss Chatto even more after the bird-balloon incident.

Chapter 4
Ren

The morning after the fire, we had to wear the same clothes again. All we had was in the carrier bags.

We sat on the bed. At home I loved looking over at the tree close to my bedroom window. Now, through the milky glass, we looked out at some bins. After we were dressed, Mum and Dad were ringing people and talking in hushed voices. "This is a nightmare," I heard Mum say.

Last night she had said we were lucky, but I think the luck had drained away.

My stomach kept churning and churning and

Mum and Dad kept talking on their phones and then to each other and then back on their phones again. I had some sweets in the bottom of my fleece pocket. I gave one to Petie so he wouldn't whinge.

They didn't really talk to us. There were loads of people to tell and the business to sort out. It was a huge mess because they'd been pitching for a big contract that would start in a couple of months' time, and now they might miss out.

"It's unthinkable," Dad said. He kept being put on hold and swearing. "We need an appointment now. Yes, I'll hold on. Can we come in and see someone about that? Is there someone available? No, we're in rented accommodation. The address. Hang on a minute."

Petie kept asking me things I couldn't answer. And stupid things. "Where's the special breakfast?" he asked.

I shrugged.

"Dad!" Petie grabbed Dad's arm.

Dad swung round and paused from tapping on his phone. "What?"

"Ren said there was a special breakfast."

Dad sighed. "We'll get you some breakfast in a minute."

"What about school?" I asked.

Mum rolled her eyes. "Not today," she said. "Not on top of everything else!"

We waited. We peered out of the milky window again. Below us were grey paving slabs and bins piled up with packaging. There was a broken vacuum cleaner leaning up against a bin. And a picture frame.

Petie nudged me. A rat had gone to sit on one of the bin lids. It started clawing round the lid, sticking its head inside. Its long tail waved about like a rope. It dived inside and the lid flipped shut.

We looked at each other.

"Let's get it out, Ren," Petie said. "It's trapped. Let's go and help it?"

"No," I said. "You shouldn't help rats."

"Why?"

"They aren't clean."

"That's not their fault. We could go down and prop the lid open."

"Then more rats might come," I said. I still wanted the rat to come back out, though. He must be squashed in there with all the rubbish.

"What are you both staring at?" Mum asked.

"A rat."

"What?" Mum pulled Petie away from the window. "This place," she murmured.

"We have to go down and help the rat," Petie wailed.

"Right. That's it. Out. Now!" Mum said.

Ten seconds later we had locked our rooms and we were on our way down the road.

✗

We had breakfast in a café. I had hot chocolate, toast and jam. Petie kept flopping down on the seat and sliding under the table.

"He's overtired," Mum said.

"It's going to be a long day," Dad murmured.

The woman behind the till kept staring at us. Dad still tapped messages on his phone. Petie sprawled against me and I kept flopping him back up against Dad.

I chewed my toast slowly. It didn't taste of much. Maybe my mouth had breathed too much smoke to taste properly. I took a long time to drink the hot chocolate. I dropped some bits of the toast into the cup and watched them float and soak up the wet until they sank. I fished them out with a spoon and sucked them between my teeth.

Now Mum was on her phone too. She leapt up.

"I'll take this call outside," she murmured to Dad.

"Shall I clear away?" the till lady asked. She was still staring at me. The side of her top lip twitched. She folded her arms like cross teachers do.

"Leave it," Dad said. "The kids are still eating."

My hot chocolate had turned to chocolate soup. Cold. Like weird baby food.

"I don't want it now," I said to Dad.

"What have you *done* to it?"

"The toast wasn't very nice."

"OK, OK." Dad stacked the plates. "We're done!"

Chapter 5
Ren

We drove home.

The place that had been our house was behind cones wrapped round with orange tape. There were notices saying, *Danger* and *Keep Out*. Petie and me stared, standing in exactly the same place where we had been last night.

Now it wasn't on fire any more, our ruined house looked like a drawing in a book where a giant hand had torn a hole to scoop out some people to eat. The hoses had gone. It wasn't smoking any more because everything was wet. The beams that used to make the roof were black twig shapes crisscrossing in the sky, like broken ladders to nowhere.

"Keep hold of Petie's hand," Mum said. "Dad and I have lots to sort out. Well done, love."

Mum and Dad talked to a fireman and Dad went through the tape with him into the garden at the side where rubble and beams made mounds.

"We've finished damping it down. We're satisfied it won't ignite again," I heard the fireman say.

A man in orange overalls arrived and a person in white overalls took photos.

Petie's hand squirmed inside mine. His sharp little nails pushed into my palm. "I want to go in. Can we go inside?"

"No. We have to stand here."

"Can we move those orange things?"

"No!"

My eyes travelled up to my ripped-in-half bedroom with the floor tipping away so you could see layers of floorboards, chunks of brick and blackened wallpaper. I looked up at the thin torn curtains and the crumbled-away walls. I could still see some of the clouds with rainbows tucked in behind them. I couldn't help picturing my collections of interesting little things in their boxes and cases; were all my little animals smashed and gone? They couldn't *all* have melted or broken, could they? Maybe a fireman had scooped up some?

Inside me, I felt all smashed and wrong too, smoked out, like they did with the wasps' nest in our garden to finish off the wasps.

We walked round the outside of the tape and looked down our garden. The tree outside my window lay on its side, poking out from under a pile of bricks and broken beams. Two firemen were raking the charred remains. I saw one putting things in a bag. Maybe some were my things. Maybe they had found some animals or ornaments from my collections. Or maybe the whole cupboard had been saved. It was a good cupboard with a lock and a little silver key. It had been a birthday present with my name on, painted by Mum's friend. I didn't really want to just leave it … if it was lying somewhere in the garden. It was colourful. If it was there, I thought I would see it. Although … maybe it was underneath something.

Mrs Elton from next door appeared beside us and put her arm round Petie. "So sorry," she said in a shaky voice. She clutched me too. "Poor little things," she said.

Dad and the overall man waved Mum over. Mum's and Dad's voices were hushed but I could still hear.

I heard the man say, "We need to make the site secure," and "Have you spoken to your insurer?"

"Yes, they're sending someone down."

"We shouldn't have brought the kids." Mum's voice sounded flat and far away.

The downstairs room beside the kitchen was just a pile. That was Mum and Dad's study. The man walking round with Mum was saying that the fire had started there. *That's where the heat was greatest. No chance of retrieving any of the equipment.*

"Some seriously big bits of tech by the look of the remains," he said.

"That's our home office. We run a business. Mail order."

Mum and Dad looked at each other, their faces screwed up.

"How much did you have backed up?" Dad hissed to Mum.

"Some… Not all of it," she said.

"Will the insurers pay out?" Dad asked the overall man.

"Depends on the level of cover you had. And the

cause of the fire," the man said. "These things can take a long while to sort out."

"We were about to land our biggest contract," Dad said. "The timing couldn't be worse. What a mess. What a total mess. How on earth are we going to…?"

Mum shook her head. "Not in front of the kids! We can't stay. It's not good for them." Her hand clamped round my arm. "Come on, you two."

Dad waved to the man. "I'll be back. Two o'clock. Yep."

"Are any of our things OK?" I asked.

"There might be a few. They'll bring them round." Mum saw my face. "But your bedroom took the biggest impact, love, because the fire began in our office, directly underneath it. There were very high temperatures. Don't get your hopes up." She walked us both back to the car. "We're all OK. That's what matters."

Dad pulled open the car door. "Where's your mum?" Mum asked him. "I thought you said she was meeting us here?"

"Only if she could make it. If not, I said we would go round to hers."

"Well, she's not here."

"She's been away for the weekend."

"She's always away." Mum sounded cross now.

Dad was cross back. "She wasn't to know we'd have a crisis!"

"I need the loo," Petie said.

"Why didn't you go in the café?"

"I didn't need to in the café." He waved back at our broken house. "Shall we see if the toilet is still there?"

"We can't," Dad said.

"Why?"

"The bricks that made the house are not safe. They'll … they'll have to pull the rest of it down," Dad said.

"And then build it again?" Petie said brightly.

"Yes," Mum said. She glanced at Dad. "Build it again. Get in the car. We're going to Gran's. You can use the loo there."

"Will they bring all our things round to Gran's?"

"No, Petie. We'll have to get new things."

Petie began to cry. "But I like our old things."

"I know," Mum said. "Come on."

We piled in. Gran lived on the other side of town. I sat listening to Mum and Dad and watching all the cars. Normally I would be at school, but nothing was normal.

"What about the tenders for the contract?" Dad asked Mum.

"I was only partway through them," she said.

"How long have we got to get it done?"

"Four or five weeks. Six weeks tops." Mum put her hand to her head, covering her eyes. "It's unbelievable!"

Petie sagged against me.

We were leaving home behind and lots of other things seemed to be in a mess too. But what was the mess about? Mum and Dad had said that we were lucky, but they didn't seem to think we were lucky now. They seemed to think the opposite.

Chapter 6
Caspar

I decided I would find out everyone's birthdays in my class. Not everyone announces when it's their birthday, although some people have badges or they come in the room with a special expression, hoping you'll notice, like *Hey, everyone, ask me about today.*

I love birthdays. My brother Matty's going to come back for my next birthday – he promised as he was leaving to go to uni. "I'll find you a present in Edinburgh!" he had said.

He might come sooner, though. He wasn't sure of his plans.

If you think about your birthday, it's a bit like you're living that day in capital letters. You want the best things to happen. And they should. Other people want it too if they like you. I would never agree to have a dentist appointment on my birthday. Imagine leaping out of bed and saying to Mum and Dad, "What are we doing today?" and they go "Special day! Yippee! Orthodontist!"

I'm not being rude or anything. I have to see the orthodontist a lot. Dr Finch is a really nice lady. I don't know why I started talking about my orthodontist. Sometimes ideas run away with me. Anyway, if I made a birthday list, that would mean I could shout *happy birthday* in school and probably be the first to say it and then lots of people around me would say to the person, *Oh, is it your birthday?* and the room would warm up with everyone joining in. It would be a good way to start the day. And with thirty of us, that's a lot of good days. I suppose some birthdays would be at the weekends. In that case, I thought, maybe I could shout it as the person was leaving on a Friday.

I started the list and then a thing happened and everyone knew everyone's birthday all at once anyway because all the dates were put on a timeline. It was for a good reason, though. It was for an art project. The artist came in to tell us about it. My whole year group were going to be doing it.

Miss Chatto introduced him. "So, everyone, this is Jake Di Gambo. Welcome, Jake." Miss Chatto's eyes gleamed when she was excited.

"This is a lovely chance for you to create something special as a class. There'll be an exhibition. I'm so pleased he chose to work with our year group."

The artist wore a long, green leather coat. I thought he looked a bit like a pirate with his beard. Artists usually dress in bold clothes; I've noticed that. I wondered where he had bought that long green coat because it was very unusual. But then, when he started to speak, it all flew out of my mind because he was exciting. Much more than most teachers you see every day. He was just so enthusiastic. And he sat on Miss Chatto's desk, just shunted back all the books and pen pots and perched. Schools don't usually have people in them who perch on desks. Jake was rare, I told Dad when he picked me up later.

And then the actual project was explained to us.

"This project is called *My Life in a Box*," Jake said. "I want to explore what things make you the person you are. What makes you tick?"

He had a low voice. His eyes fixed on you. When he said *tick* his finger did a sort of flick, as if he was conducting an orchestra and all the players were watching his hands ready to play their instruments.

A lot of us were born in May. More than you would expect, Miss Chatto said. "Isn't that funny. My birthday's in May too." She filled it in on the timeline and Jake put his on there too.

Soon the whole page was packed with all our names and birthdays.

"We've missed one off," I said. "Ren's away. Does anyone know when Ren's birthday is?"

"We'll add it later," Miss Chatto said.

We all brainstormed important objects in our lives. Finn and me made a list for five minutes then Jake collected everyone's ideas on a flip chart.

"First toy – a pull-along truck," I said. Matty got it for me. I think it was mostly him pulling it and me watching him.

"Something you use for a hobby – rollerblades," Finn said. "Something you've made. We made a marble run. It was epic."

I kept remembering objects from when I was really small, like my leaping wooden frog. I didn't even know where that was now. Probably broken and thrown away.

"If you like cats, could you put your cat in the box?" Hannah asked.

"A picture of one," Jake said.

"That's what I meant."

"Clothes. Lucky socks," Mishe said.

"Can they be valuable things?" Theo asked.

Jake laughed. "All your boxes will make up an exhibition in school, so better not put in your gran's engagement ring."

"Imagine putting in the Crown Jewels," Theo said.

"Hey, I like that idea. What would the King put in a box, everyone?" Jake asked. "Bet he'd have a lot to choose from."

Finn was still making his list. "Video games. PlayStation, Xbox..."

Jake grinned. "You could take a picture of some technology or write why you love it, but don't bring it in. You guys would just sit there playing it. Other rules?" he said. "Any suggestions?"

"Don't put in things that are alive," someone said.

"So no stick insects or pets?" Theo asked. "But can we put in dead things?"

Jake pursed his lips for a second. "I think ... no."

"What about something that's nearly dead?" Theo asked.

Everyone looked at him. I wondered what Jake would say.

"What have you got in mind, Theo?"

"I don't know," he said.

"If you're not sure, come and ask me or show me the thing and I'll give you an answer. OK?"

He could have said don't ask stupid questions. But he didn't. I liked the way Jake answered. He took us seriously and really listened.

Thinking of characters and what they might put in a box was just the best afternoon! We sat brainstorming. What would people with particular jobs put in a box?

"Scientist," I said. "So ... test tube."

"Qualifications," said Finn.

"Microscope ... slide ... weird green slime," I said.

We drew our favourite objects to go in different boxes, cut them out and stuck them on big sheets on the walls.

Jake gave us ideas and then let us try things. I stuck my new bug species on the wall then walked in a big loop around the classroom, looking at everyone else's work.

"That's brilliant," I told Grace. She was drawing a golden carriage the King would have. Then I watched Shabbir drawing a hat with a huge purple feather for an actor. "That's a clever idea," I said.

"What are you doing, Caspar?" Miss Chatto asked. "Why are you out of your seat?"

"I'm enjoying this too much to stay in one place," I said. "And I wanted to tell Shabbir I liked his actor's hat."

"Go back and sit down now."

"Can I go the long way back?"

"No."

"This is such a good afternoon. I think this is the best afternoon we've had for weeks."

"Thank you, Caspar. Can I have everyone

listening for a minute, please?" Miss Chatto said.

"I also think—"

"That's enough, Caspar. Back in your seat, please."

"You have so many great ideas," Jake told our class. "We're all bound to do this project differently. There's no one and only way. Start thinking about your own box now and listing ideas. What do you care about? What sums you up as a person?"

He grinned. "I'm glad you're enjoying what we're doing, Caspar."

He had very alive eyes. He reminded me of a lemur.

"I'm very inspired," I told him. "I'm going to do more box ideas at home."

"Great!"

"Do you go into other schools like ours?" I asked.

"This is the first time we've done the *My Life in a Box* project actually."

Miss Chatto had her hand up for silence. "That means quiet," I told Jake.

He nodded. "Beaut."

Chapter 7
Ren

After visiting our burned house, we went to my gran's. Gran lived on her own. She had a divorce from my grandad ages and ages ago and now Grandad lives in Spain.

She met us at the door. Gran is a smart sort of person. "Come on in. Shoes off."

She hugged us. "What a mess," she said. "I got the first train I could." We all went through to the kitchen. Gran's house smelled strongly of flowery air freshener. "What are they saying about the house?" she asked Dad.

"It's gutted, Mum," Dad said. "It's an insurance

job now. Could take weeks to even get a price for a rebuild."

Gran nodded, looking at me. "Get the kids back to school."

"We will. There's just a lot to sort out."

"Bit of normality."

"Yes, we know that."

"Right, so—"

"Look, Mum, is there any chance...?" Dad began saying.

Gran held up her hand and her eyes darted to Petie and me.

"How about you two watch some TV?" Mum said. "Is that OK, Stella?"

"It's inside the wooden unit in the living room. The remote's on the table," Gran said.

"Why is the TV hiding?" Petie asked as we made our way through.

I guessed the grown-ups had sent us out so they could whisper more plans. We sat on the sofa watching cartoons. A bear was chasing a rabbit across a field. The bear was massive. Its huge paws pounded the ground. The rabbit was fleeing to its burrow. It hid behind a tree and made itself thin, but the bear came round the other side and swiped with a paw full of sharp claws *Whoosh.* The rabbit leapt and ran, its legs going so fast they were a blur. It ran to a cliff and stopped. It was scared of falling. As it froze there, the bear caught up, jumped on it and squashed it.

"When are we going home, Ren?" Petie asked.

"I don't know," I said, watching the bear sitting on the rabbit and the rabbit's eyes rolling.

"Could we live at Lisa's house?" Petie asked.

Lisa was Mum's friend.

"She's only got one bedroom," I said. "That won't work."

"So where *will* we go?"

"I don't know."

I was tired of the cartoons. They were too bright and flickery. I closed my eyes and tried to remember the things in my bedroom that I'd loved the best: my kite on the back of my door, my elephant with jewel eyes, my glass cat with the curled tail, my pottery mouse. My eyes felt very heavy. Gran's sofa wasn't a curling-up kind. It had hard arms. I wanted to lie on the floor on the rug but Gran's house felt like the wrong kind of house for that, so in the end I curled round a cushion. The day was long, sad and edgy. I kept remembering what happened to our house with a jolt.

x

It was our second night in the B&B and Mum and Dad waited for Petie to fall asleep.

"We've got things to sort out, Ren, and you and Petie need to sleep," Dad whispered. "We'll just be in the room next door." Then the door swished shut.

I lay in the dark. I think the walls must have been very thin. I could hear Mum and Dad. There was stress in their voices, clipped words: *but we can't … we'll have to ask … and if she says no…*

I fell asleep.

I woke in the dark. Something was jabbing me. Petie's bony elbow. "Ren! Where's Mum?"

"In the loo," I muttered.

If I told him Mum was sleeping next door, he would get upset. This way he would go back to sleep.

"I don't like this bed. It smells wrong." Petie wriggled and turned with his arms spread out. This time he hit me in the face.

"Oi!" I whacked him away. "Move back to your own side!"

He rolled away. A few minutes passed. He rolled back towards me. His hand tugged my hair. "Ren, Ren, where's Mr Softie?" he moaned.

Mr Softie was his little soft bear from his bed at home.

I was properly awake now. "I don't know," I said, which wasn't true because anyone could guess. I didn't want any questions like that, but Petie held on to me in the dark. His fingers came round my neck. "You're choking me!"

His grip loosened. "But is Mr Softie still in our house? Shall we ask a fireman to look for him?"

How stupid! That little bear was bound to be burned and gone. "No," I said. "The firemen have gone home. Go to sleep."

Petie lay in silence for a moment, then his voice came again in the dark. "Mr Softie won't be asleep. Not without me."

I wished Mum and Dad were here. I wished I hadn't lied about Mum being in the loo. Petie kept clutching me. "Tell me where Mr Softie is!"

If Petie wants something, you give in in the end. Mum and Dad do. He was never going to sleep without an answer.

Think of something – he won't know.

"Maybe," I said, "maybe Mr Softie went for a walk before the fire started and … and he saw the flames. 'I'm not going back in there,' he said and

… and … he jumped in the tree – you know the one, outside my bedroom."

I thought of the tree, all black and charred. That wouldn't have helped him much!

Petie's hand went still on my neck. "So where is he now then, Ren … Ren?" His voice went smaller. "Did his fur get burned?"

Now what?

"No, no, he was … the only thing that stayed perfect. He jumped to safety."

"Jumped to safety," Petie repeated. "I knew it. I knew he would. And then?"

"Um, a bird came and rescued him. The bird took him up and away."

Petie did a joyful little wriggle. "Away where?"

I had run out of ideas. "I'll tell you tomorrow."

"But, Ren…"

"He's all right. I'll tell you some more tomorrow."

Petie sighed. "G'night, Ren." He snuggled into me all hot and soon he was breathing soft and long again.

I lay awake for ages. Someone should have read Petie a story. Well, that wasn't going to happen; we didn't have any books now!

Chapter 8
Caspar

We were well on the way with the *My Life in a Box* project.

"So, I want you to think about what should go in a box about *you*," Jake said. "This list might help. How about: something you love to wear, pictures of family and friends, things you have made, things from your hobbies, objects from when you were really small, favourite sports kit, anything you love to collect… They need to be things that will fit in a shoebox or similar. Of course, it doesn't have to be a box. Come up with whatever feels right to you that most reflects who you are. Be as creative as you can."

Miss Chatto showed us her tap shoes from her dancing classes and the skirt she wore to dance in.

Jake showed us his sketchbooks.

We all wrote down ideas and thought about how we would decorate our boxes.

"Sky's the limit!" Jake said. "I'm hoping some of you will tell us about your choices in the weeks ahead. I'm just really excited to see what you guys produce."

"Can we make two boxes?" I asked. "One box doesn't seem enough!"

Later on, as I was leaving, I met Jake in the corridor. "Do you live near here?" I asked him.

"No. I'm staying with my brother while I do the project with you guys."

"Oh," I said. "I've got a brother. He's in Edinburgh."

"Wow," Jake said. "Well, that's cool."

Chapter 9
Ren

"Gather up your things," Mum said. "We're on the move."

"Where are we going?"

"Gran's."

We had never stayed at Gran's before, even though we had always lived quite near her. Maybe we stayed with her when we were babies, but I don't think so.

"We don't have to be in the B&B any more. Hooray!" we shouted and jumped on the bed and things were falling off on the floor. "No more rat!"

"It's incredibly generous," Dad said.

"How will we all fit in?" I asked.

"That's the clever bit," Mum said.

We drove to Gran's on the other side of town. Since we had visited yesterday someone had parked a caravan on Gran's drive. It was the kind you tow on a holiday.

"We're borrowing it from Liv and Ellie," Mum said. Liv and Ellie were old friends of Mum's.

"Wow. Petie, we're going to be in a caravan!"

Petie and I rushed up to it. I remembered when we once went on a holiday and stayed in a caravan park with another family, right by the sea, and we spent all our time on the beach or cooking together in the little garden.

I jumped on the platform step. "Can we go inside it? Please!"

Mum unlocked the door and we looked in and inside was a table with a laptop on it and some piles of folders. We jumped up the steps. "Where are the beds?" I asked, looking around.

"The bed folds down," Mum said. She was still standing outside, frowning.

Something stirred inside me. I started to feel a cooler thing. "So … where do we all sleep?"

Mum shook her head. "Look, Ren, love, the best

thing is for you and Petie to sleep in the house."

"What? No!"

"Yes, I'm sorry, love, but Dad and I will be sleeping in the caravan."

"We want the caravan. We want the caravan!" I chanted, and Petie joined in.

"Ren, love, there's no possibility of you two being outside in the caravan by yourselves and there isn't room for all four of us."

There must be a way, I thought. "We'll take it in turns being with you, won't we, Petie?" I said. "I'll have Monday, Wednesday and Friday, and Petie can have the other days."

"No."

"But…"

"No, Ren. It won't work. Dad and I need to work late on things for the business. The caravan will be like our office. I'm sorry, love. You're much better inside with Gran."

My heart was wrenching. "That's just wrong."

"Come in the house and see."

We took our shoes off, put them on the shoe rack and followed Mum upstairs. I was realising something as we got to the top of the stairs. There were only two bedrooms and if Gran was already in one…

"Hopefully it won't be for too long," Mum said brightly.

The bedroom had two single beds, each one with a cupboard beside it. Plain brown duvets, cream-coloured rug down the middle and a picture on the wall of a teapot and a cup and saucer with a pot of flowers. It didn't seem like an actual person's room; it was a brown spare room.

"Let's get you unpacked, then we can all sit in the garden. We're so lucky to have this offer from Gran. It's extremely kind," Mum said again.

I realised Gran had come to stand in the doorway behind Mum. "I'm sure you'll get used to it," she said. "And I'll be only just along the landing."

I don't know if her being along the landing was meant to be a good thing or whether she meant *watch out.*

It wasn't like the B&B was nicer, but it still felt odd. Gran just stood there outside the doorway, frowning in a navy-blue padded jacket.

"There's a cupboard each. You've both got exactly the same so there won't be any need for arguments," she said. She sounded like a person who is worried you're going to wreck everything.

She didn't want us in her house.

"No need for arguments!" Dad called from the stairs. "You don't know these two. They could argue about whether grass is green."

"Oh," Gran said. She wasn't smiling.

Chapter 10
Ren

On our first night in the brown spare room, I jerked awake to find Petie pushing his way under the duvet and into my bed.

"Hey… What? … Petie, WHAT ARE YOU DOING?!"

"I can't sleep," he said.

"Well, I can." I tried to turn but my arm was trapped underneath him. I pulled it out. "You have to go back to your own bed."

"But I can't."

I knew what was coming.

"Ren, where is Mr Softie? You said … you said

you'd tell me."

Now what to do? "He's on holiday," I said, trying to think of how to stop having this conversation. "He's gone a long way away … on a plane."

Petie gasped. "A plane!"

"Yes. And now he's … far … far away." I yawned.

Maybe Petie would stop now. His breath was hot beside my face. His fingers scratched at my arm. "He should come home," he said. "I want him to come home. Shall we go and get him?"

Now what? "No, because someone else has got him," I said quickly.

"Who?" Petie's voice was sharp and shocked.

"A girl. She saw him when he left the airport and she put him in her backpack."

"That's like me. That's what I do," Petie said happily.

"Yes, that's it."

I began to turn over. "Ren!"

"What now?"

"What's the girl's name?"

I thought quickly. "Flynn."

"Flynn can't have him for ever." Petie's voice was a bleat.

"No, she knows that."

"Where did she take him?"

"To her house."

His voice was a soft breath. "Where?"

Now what should I say? Think of a place … far away. The picture that used to hang in our kitchen… The mountain range in Switzerland.

"Mr Softie's far away in … in the Alps," I said.

"Oooh." Petie breathed out fast by my ear. "He won't like it."

I pulled away. "He might like being on holiday."

Petie stretched and lay still. Then his little voice came again. "Does he miss me?"

The air seemed to wait for my answer. "Um … yes." I didn't want to tell the story any more. "I don't know anything else," I said. "Stop asking."

Petie was a big wriggly hot lump. It was my bed. He was an invader. Why did I have to make up stories in the middle of the night?

"Will you tell me some more tomorrow?"

All these questions! "Yes, but only if you go back and get in your bed."

I felt him pull away and watched his dark shape pad back across the carpet.

Then he was quiet. After a while, his breathing went softer.

I lay with my eyes open, staring at the brown picture with the cup and the flowers on the plain cream-coloured wall. I'd lied to Petie. So what? Think how terrible it would be if I'd told him the truth.

Chapter 11
Caspar

Our class trooped into the art gallery to look at the portraits. Some of them were really old. The gallery woman said that long ago they didn't used to have photographs so when they wanted to paint a portrait of themselves, people sat with a mirror propped up and painted or drew themselves from that. This had never occurred to me before. It blew my mind. She said people used to put objects in the picture to show what they loved or cared about, like maybe a little dog or some books.

"What would you put beside you in your self-portrait?" Jake asked us, leaning against the wall. Jake always seemed to be very excited by things. His eyes shone. "Think … what makes you who you are?"

I actually would have liked to put my bike in my portrait but bikes are hard to draw. My dog, Snaffle, I decided. He would take up the whole picture. I could be peeping out from behind his fur.

Theo said he would put a fat rat in and everyone laughed.

I said, "That's not something you love, is it, Theo?"

And he said, "I'll put in what I like, you coffee pot."

I don't get why that's funny. It isn't. How can a person be a coffee pot? They can't. So why did everyone laugh?

Miss Chatto said *shush* and most people did, except Theo, who kept saying stupid suggestions under his breath. He's always doing that.

An ermine was a kind of weasel, Miss Chatto said. Look. You could see the brush strokes on the portrait of a woman holding the ermine. She had very beautiful flowing clothes.

"Why's she holding that weasel?" I asked.

"Well, Caspar, it was probably a pet," Miss Chatto said.

Everyone else moved on to look at the next portrait but I stayed staring at the weasel woman. She didn't look very happy. Her mouth turned down at the sides and she looked a bit worn out. Maybe looking after a weasel made you very tired. The great thing was the clothes she had on were so well painted they looked completely real. And the weasel's fur looked exactly like real fur. You could see places where it was flat and you felt as if you could almost stretch out your hand to stroke it. I think the artist was really good.

"That was a great trip!" I said, when we were leaving. "I think everyone enjoyed it. Thank you."

"Glad you liked it, Caspar," Jake said. I liked that he used my name. "You're good at really looking hard at the pictures, not just rushing past. I like that," he said.

"And I like your coat," I said. "I'm glad I've got a dog and not an ermine. Why did you become an artist?"

"Oh, I think I've just always loved making things," he said.

"My brother's going to be an engineer. That's what he really loves."

"You always tell me about your brother. What about you, Caspar? What are you going to be?"

"Oh, I don't know. I'm quite an alert person. I wondered if I might make a good spy," I said.

*

At home I wandered around, but I couldn't really start work on things or finish other things. Dad had found me some wrapping paper to go round my box and I'd made some stencils to print round the edge, but it wasn't so much fun on my own. Normally I would have got Matty's ideas. Maybe he would even have found some things to go in my box. At least we could have chatted about it. We used to talk every day after school.

"What's up, love?" Mum asked when she saw me lying on the floor hugging Snaffle.

"I haven't got any ideas."

"You've always got ideas. I thought you were really excited about your box project?"

"I am. I'm just... Matty hasn't rung for three days."

"Come here." Mum reached out and hugged me. "Look, love, Matty's probably just getting used to his new life."

"I still don't get it. Couldn't he just ring to say hello, like, for two minutes?"

Mum smiled. "I'm sure he'll call at the weekend."

My brother Matty was very good at making things. At weekends sometimes he was sleeping in and I was in my room and all of a sudden a huge shape would come flying towards me and he would jump on me, calling, "Come on, Pipsqueak. What are we doing today?" I didn't mind that he called me Pipsqueak. It wasn't in a mean way. He had always called me that.

He used to invent things we could make from bits in the shed mixed with things he collected from skips in local streets. He would have come up with something really amazing for my box. He just would. I wanted him to ring so I could tell him about it.

When Snaffle was really small, we made a mini dog show with lots of dogs from our street and tickets for sale. They had to weave in and out of an obstacle course we made from clothes racks, ladders and cardboard. It was hilarious. Sometimes when our plans collapsed Matty said, "Well, we won't try that again!" We had made some really stupid inventions. But now he was gone, I could see it was mostly him having the ideas and me collecting the stuff. I was good for reading out labels because Matty's eyes weren't as good as mine. He was like Mum and I was like Dad. He was always craning and blinking and saying, "What does it say on that packet?" So I was useful.

When you have a brother who is eight years older, it's like you are never going to catch up. Matty had always seemed huge and just really clever. When I was two he was ten, so I would just stare up at this huge grinning person who swung me round. I was always watching him. He's good at sports and we went to watch him play on Saturday mornings. When I was five, his team won the league and I remember jumping up and down and cheering so much that the *Go, Matty, Go* banner I had made ripped in two. He put me on his shoulders and said to his mates that I could be their mascot. He was Matty and I was Pipsqueak. I was like a speck compared to him.

He didn't just do everything before me; he did it years before me, which is good for me, he said, because Mum and Dad were different with me than most parents and forgot that I was a lot younger.

Our house seemed very quiet now. Now no one came hurtling into my room.

We weren't fun without Matty. I didn't know what to do without him.

Chapter 12
Ren

When we moved to Gran's, we had just supermarket bags for our things. I had discovered a few things of ours in the mesh bag at the back of the car seat: sweets, a hair scrunchie, a book of puzzles. But there was nothing special, nothing I cared about.

Petie and me didn't know where to go in Gran's house. When we arrived, there were lots of lamps and china ornaments – proper smart things with places where you should put them back. There wasn't any dust. Maybe Gran frightened it away. Everything had edges and polished bits. There were gleaming pieces of furniture, mirrors everywhere, green plants with shiny leaves, jugs of flowers, mats and ornaments, like one of a lady on a swing with a sticking-out dress.

There were more rules at Gran's than there were at school.

Don't touch the plants, brush against them or even stroke them. Don't run. Walk nicely and sit in sitting rooms. Food is to eat in the kitchen, or the dining room if it's a special meal. No TV. Screen time only for homework. The garden had little paths and a grassy lawn but you couldn't play football. I felt a bit like someone had put us in a cage and that made me want to run more.

In Gran's kitchen we only smashed a cup and a plate in the first week. Mum said she would replace them but then Gran bought some different cups and plates with pink birds on made from some kind of plastic that was dishwasher safe. Indestructible, Dad said. I hated those pink birds; they were yuck.

Just for a new place to be, I peeped inside Gran's bedroom at the end of the landing. There was polished wood furniture, a big old bed with a flowery cover and, in the corner, a little glass-fronted cupboard like a bookcase. But it didn't have books in. Little objects sparkled on the shelves.

"Ren!" Mum's voice came from downstairs. I turned away and ran out of the room. I would come back. I would explore it another time.

I had been right; sharing the brown spare room with Petie was really bad. He wouldn't stay on his side. I made a chopping machine with my legs and if he crossed the line where the carpet had a ridge, he would get chopped. "You will be in tiny bits, so watch out," I said.

Petie's bedroom at home had been full of plastic rubbish. He never really played anyway, just smashed the toys against each other and said, "Now you're dead." That's not playing. At Gran's he had some new plastic toys and they were all over the floor *again*. I had already told Dad, and he said I should be *understanding*, and that Petie wasn't used to sharing a room, but that's not a good argument because I wasn't used to it either. I couldn't even walk across the floor without catching my foot on a plastic animal or a car. We fought about the line and Petie did sudden tiny moves, crossing it, then leaping back again with this insane grin. I screamed, "*Get off the line!*" and he screamed back, "*I'm not on it, you ratbag!*", waving his legs into my bit of the room.

I ran downstairs and wrenched open the caravan door. "I can't be with Petie!" I shouted.

The caravan was filled with equipment now: screens and PCs. Mum leapt up from behind a screen. She had headphones on and pushed one to the side. "Ren, you'll have to hang on, love. I'm on a call. I'll try to pop into the house soon," she said in a busy sort of voice.

"Where's Dad?"

"At the bank. We'll have a chat at bedtime. See if you can sort it out yourself." She put the headphone back and said something.

I still stood there. "I can't sort it out myself," I said.

"Last time I called you, you put me through to your customer service line. I want your small business service..." Mum didn't even look at me. She'd forgotten I was there. "I understand that but ... I know that but ... I've already given those details to your colleague... Ah, finally." Mum saw me still there and cupped her hand over her phone. "This is really important, Ren. Go inside and I'll come and find you soon." Then, into the phone, "Sorry, yes, I am here... The Cardinal Avenue fire.

Yes, I've emailed you the loss adjuster's findings. Look, I can't solve this if you keep…" She held the phone away from her. "Go inside, Ren."

I wandered back inside. How was I supposed to sort this out? This bedroom was impossible.

I had tried making a line with tape. "This is your bit and this is my bit," I told Petie. "If your things are in my bit, they may be removed and destroyed." That's what they say at stations and on trains.

I marched back into the room and the whole floor was full of Petie and his bits of games and toys like a snowdrift.

I stood over him. "Move your things on to your side!"

Petie looked up. "I don't care, dooby-doo, you are a poo!" he sang.

A very angry feeling flared up in me and I said, "I will grind your animals into tiny flakes and throw the bits in the river."

Something was going to happen. I breathed in and started screaming right up near his face. "Go awayeeeeeeeeeeee!"

Petie covered his ears and screamed back still with that stupid, stupid grin. "No wayeeeeeeeeeeeee!"

We both screamed flat out. My lungs were

burning. I felt my face boil. I clenched my fists. I pushed the breath until it was all gone and we both stopped and panted. I dived on to my bed and pulled the duvet over me. I was shaking. My body felt hot and empty and worn out. We were like wild animals, like creatures in a documentary. After a while I peeped out. Petie's face was right there peeping in at me through a gap under the duvet. We both burst out laughing.

This turned into our new thing at Gran's. Any time we were cross, we did the screaming. No one ever came and nothing ever happened. It was better than hitting and the winner was the one with the most breath who was still screaming when the other one ran out of puff, and that was nearly always me.

Sometimes one of us would try to pop the other's balloon of breath by suddenly squashing their chest. One time Petie threw some water at me from a glass by the bed. I gasped, cold and soaked. That ended the screaming that time. Another time Petie stopped and did a big burp and said, "I'm feeling sick," and we both waited to see if he would be and then we didn't feel like carrying on. Mostly, though, we screamed until we were screamed out.

✗

At teatimes Dad said he would try to come out from the caravan to join us. He didn't always make it, though. Sometimes we had meals with just Gran and us. Gran's food was very bad. Often it was covered in gravy and it smelled terrible.

One evening Petie said, "Oh no," when the chicken came out. "Why did she put the brown sauce stuff on the chicken?"

I tried a bit. It caught in my throat and made me choke. It was completely disgusting.

"You're lucky to have homemade food," Gran said.

"I can't eat it," I said.

"It's like poo," Petie said.

Gran clattered the spoon down. "That is rude when someone has made you a meal."

"We don't eat food like this," I said. It was torture. My mouth wouldn't open any more. All the tasting parts of my tongue and cheeks were pushing my lips out. "This has gone off," I said.

"My food has not *gone off*," Gran said. "It was made today. It takes a long time to prepare a meal from scratch."

"It should go in a bin," I said.

Gran rubbed the sides of her forehead. "Eat the broccoli then," she snapped. "Eat something and go upstairs."

So we did.

Chapter 13
Ren

People gave us their things: clothes and shoes. They weren't like presents in wrapping paper. They were in bags or sometimes handed to us in the playground. When I was waiting to go into school, Amal's mum held a navy puffer coat against me. "Try this," she said, plunging my arms into sleeves and zipping it right up to my neck. I stuck my arms out, feeling sort of stuffed. She rolled back the cuffs and stood back. "Perfect for the winter. You'll soon grow into it," she said. "Don't worry, I've washed it."

"Thanks ever so much," Mum said.

Mum had told us to say thank you and we did. It's hard to explain but the things didn't feel like ours because we didn't choose them. No one said what would you like; they just gave us what they wanted or had spare. Mum kept saying how kind everyone was and how lucky we were.

Amelia's mum had organised and collected for an art set for me. They all gave me it in the playground. It was huge, as big as my desk at school, and it had paints, felt-tips and highlighters and coloured pencils fanned out in a circle. There were so many colours. But somehow I couldn't use it. I took out all the pens and pencils and put them in a carrier bag. I felt as if they belonged to someone else. Chloe gave me a pair of bright-pink earmuffs. I do like earmuffs but these weren't really me. They'd be better for someone like Amelia, who wore lots of pink things. They were a kind of shouty object and I'm not really a shouty person.

I lay on my bed in the brown spare room and made a list of all the things that were now gone, things that I would never see any more.

My collections of little animals and glass and china things in their cupboard, of course. I tried to remember all of them one at a time.

The cover on my bed. It was patchwork. It took a whole summer to make. The design was made up of triangles and squares all in bright colours and patterns spreading out like a giant sunflower.

My art materials in their wooden box, paints and sketching things.

My hair things, clips and clasps.

My jelly stickers on the window that I made myself at art club.

My bookshelf with all my notebooks and craft kit.

Trainers.

My favourite piece of clothing: my cherry-red jacket with the hot-air balloons embroidered on the back that Mum and Dad bought for me at the Summer Fiesta. I wanted it the minute we saw it, even though it was too big. I said, "I can roll back the cuffs. Please, please. I'll wear it for years." It was pure me. I pictured the balloons, curling off the material in the fire and flying off into the clouds.

✗

Mum and Dad were always busy now we lived at Gran's house. They said Mum would be there at breakfast and sort out school things and lunches, and Dad would be there more at teatime. That turned into Mum rushing around looking for things and struggling with the kitchen.

I heard Gran say, "Just ask me, won't you, Rachel?"

Mum spun round. "Oh, I'm fine, Stella. I just haven't remembered where everything is."

"And we forgot to buy crisps," Petie said. "And the blue-packet ham. And the cheese with the red peeling bits."

"You're right," Mum said. "Sorry, love."

"I have some other types of crackers and cheese," Gran said. "Try a bit of variety in your life. Or have a banana."

"They like what they're used to," Mum said.

"Children are adaptable," Gran said.

"I'm afraid these two can be a bit picky," Mum said.

But then when Gran went out to get something, I saw Mum was rolling her eyes. "For goodness' sake…" she said, under her breath and then a swear word.

Petie and me looked at each other. Gran and Mum were like snapping things. They didn't explode; they just clipped and snapped. When they both went out of the kitchen, I flung open the food cupboard. "Quick. No one's looking!"

We stared inside at lots of jars and packets. Gran seemed to have different foods to us. I held up a jar of pale speckled beans.

"I don't want any of this stuff," Petie moaned. "All these things are wrong!"

Mum came back in. "We'll go to the shops and have our own shelf. But for now just try to eat what there is." She fixed me with a look. "I don't want this to be a thing."

"What do you want me to do?" I asked.

"Just try to help, yeah? Gran's making a massive effort for us all. And she's right really; you could try things."

Why didn't Mum say that to Petie? She was looking completely at me. Even when I tried to eat more things, no one really noticed; they just called us *these two*. I was always lumped in with Petie when it was about being picky and I wasn't as picky as he was. Not really. I thought, *Right, I won't bother, I won't bother to try to be good.* And why did Mum keep apologising for us? I didn't know we were that bad, but we must have been for Mum to be saying sorry all the time. But then, when Gran wasn't looking, Mum hissed things under her breath. She was annoyed with Gran too.

My family had turned scratchy and raw, like a cut on your knee that you keep picking at and then you crash down on and make it bleed again.

Chapter 14
Ren

We used to live round the corner from school. Now it was miles away. Living at Gran's meant we had to get the bus or go to school by car.

Gran had offered to do all the school drop-offs and pick-ups, Dad told us. "We will still see you both, but, just at the moment, we need more time to work on the contract and the paperwork about our house. We'll get more done if we don't stop," he said. "This is so kind of Gran. She'll be late for her shift at the museum, but she's keen to help us."

On our first day back at school, though, Dad took us. The day turned into a big rush. I got a massive whiff when I opened the bag with spare uniform in because someone had pushed a bottle of shampoo in there and the lid had come loose so the borrowed school skirt was damp and smelled.

When we got to school, late, Dad talked to Mrs Isaac, the deputy head, by the office, which made us even later.

I stood in the classroom doorway like a scarecrow in a wet field and Dad began talking to Miss Chatto. My class were doing silent reading. Everyone's eyes came up and there was a breath round the room, like a GASP. I heard a voice say, "She's back!"

I wanted to run out and down the road and home. I pictured the zebra crossing and imagined myself leaping along the rows of cars in Earle Gardens and arriving in our road. I blinked. That couldn't happen. Our house wasn't there any more, was it? Should I just go and sit down in my place?

Dad gave me a quick hug goodbye and left.

But instead of just telling me to sit down, Miss Chatto waved me to follow her and took me outside to the cloakroom leaving Mr Charles in charge. I heard him say, "Well, this doesn't look like silent reading to me!" And then the classroom door closed.

"Just a quick chat," Miss Chatto said. "Let's get you sorted, honey."

We both squashed in on the bench under the coats in the cloakroom. "You've had a horrible time and I'm so sorry." Miss Chatto patted her hair and smoothed the furry edge on a coat hanging beside her, like a pet. "I wanted to explain something. There's an artist, Jake Di Gambo, coming in to do a project with our class and I especially wanted to tell you about it, Ren. He introduced it to the rest of the class a few days ago. We had a visit to an art gallery. It's a real shame you missed that."

Miss Chatto was wearing one of her beautiful hairclips in her long dark hair. A tortoiseshell one with speckles of rust and dark red. It bobbed when she turned her head. "You see, honey, this project is all about who we are. We'll be making a special box and inside the box will be … there will be –" she hesitated – "things about you."

There was a horrid jolt inside me. "Everyone's making a box about *me*?"

Miss Chatto's eyes went wide. "No, no." She took out her hairclip and fiddled with it. "Goodness. No. So sorry, no, the project will be each person in the class choosing things that are special about *them*."

She wound a big ponytail round her fingers and reclipped it.

She sighed. "I thought … we thought, you could put in your memories of people … school, Ren, or places you'd like to visit."

Memories of people and school? That wouldn't work.

I stared at her excited face and shook my head. Mum's laptop with all our family photos in it was gone. We had just a few photos that had been printed out, from birthdays and when Petie was born. I pictured a photo album Mum had been given back by the fireman, the sides all damp and charred. The photos inside it were spattered with grey speckles. It's like we suddenly turned 200 years old.

Miss Chatto bit her lips. "Maybe your gran has some … photos?"

"Maybe," I said quietly. I stared at my school sweatshirt. They'd found it for me in lost property. The sweatshirt had a gluey bit on the cuff, like yoghurt or maybe actual glue.

Miss Chatto unclipped her hairclip again and made pincers with it, biting at her fingers. "Look, we'll think of things. You could … write about a holiday … and put that in your box."

I didn't know what to say. We hadn't been away on a holiday for ages. Not since Mum and Dad had started the business two years ago. They had been saving up. There had been big plans to go on holiday, maybe even to America. I gulped. Of course, those plans would be ruined now.

Miss Chatto was still suggesting things. "There might be objects you really like."

"I haven't got a room now," I blurted out. "We're at my gran's."

She nodded. "Oh, well, maybe there are a few things there?"

That brown spare room had nothing to do with me at all, not even the tiniest bit. "No," I said.

"Oh."

Miss Chatto didn't understand anything. I thought of the shopping bag with my few things inside and the clothes from Alice down the road. A box about me. I didn't even have boring or normal things. We'd even had to buy new toothbrushes!

"I'm sorry," Miss Chatto said. "You see, we planned the project before your … horrible experience. We're going to help you as much as we possibly can. You can talk to me or Jake, the artist. We'll all help find things to go in your box, I promise…"

She looked at me and did a little pleading nipped smile. I couldn't make my face smile back.

"Well … so … come and talk to me any time and the school counsellor, Marie. You could talk to her too. Now, who are you sitting with today? Amelia?"

I nodded.

"Great, great, well, I'm sure you two are good friends and she may be able to suggest ideas for your box too."

Miss Chatto stood up and, for a second, her body was lost in coats. "Whoops!" She did a little laugh. "Any time," she said softly, pushing coats to the side. "Great," she said. "Great!"

I got up and followed her back inside the classroom. And all the time I was thinking, *How is this* great*? My project will be completely the most rubbishest one in the class.*

Chapter 15
Caspar

We were standing at the bus stop when Ren appeared with her little brother and a lady I didn't know. "That's Ren," I told Dad. "She's the one from my class whose house burned down."

Some people in the queue turned to look.

"OK, Caspar," Dad said. "Don't announce it."

"I just thought it was useful for you to know," I whispered.

"It is useful," Dad murmured back.

The lady walked up to Dad, and Ren and her brother tagged along behind. The queue stepped back to let them through. They must have all felt sad about Ren's house. People don't normally let other people queue-jump.

"You're..."

"Caspar's dad," said Dad.

"Of course. I'm Ren's grandma. I've seen you in the covered market. I live in Sydney Road," she said.

"Oh, right. I was so sorry to hear about ... *the situation...*" Dad said in a low voice. "If there's anything we can do..." Their conversation went muffled as they moved round the back of the shelter.

"Don't worry, Dad," I called. "I'll keep your place. That's my dad," I told Ren. "Do you ... live near here?"

Ren sighed. "She's my gran. We're staying in her house. It's not our real house."

"Oh."

We listened to Dad and Ren's gran talking. I knew we weren't meant to so that made me listen harder.

"It's a bit of a trek, isn't it?" her grandma said.

"When we moved house, we thought, why move Caspar?" Dad told her. "It's a bit of a bind but we're hoping he'll go to St George's next year and that's only just round the corner. Some days it does get complicated with the buses. But Jeanie needs the car so ... we get on with it."

"Have you noticed my dad has grey hair and grey eyebrows, the same as your gran?" I asked.

"Oh..." Ren said. She stood stooped over, looking down at the ground. Her hands were fists.

It feels odd talking to someone who is bent over. "Oh, yeah ... and you missed the gallery visit," I said.

Ren's head came up. She nodded.

"I can tell you all about the paintings if you want?"

She tilted her head, her mouth pursed, and she looked away. That must be a no. Sometimes people just want to stand quietly. Maybe Ren was that kind of person. I didn't know her very well, even though she was in our class. My desk was near the reading corner and she sat over by the windows. I'd never worked in a group with her. I wanted to ask her about the fire but she didn't look chatty.

Instead, I talked to her brother. "What's your

name?" I asked.

"Petie."

"I used to have that backpack. I had the exact same one."

"Did you?" He grinned at me. His front tooth was missing. "Did you have this reading book?"

He dug inside his bag and pulled out his book from school. *Rabbit Bakes Biscuits.*

I laughed. "No, but I have read that book."

Ren's grandma and Dad came back to join us. "Sounds like a plan," Dad was saying. "If you're sure."

"It's better for all of us," she said. "And I won't have the early start, which I will value enormously."

The bus pulled up and we all clustered together by the doors.

"What's better for all of us?" I asked, jumping on beside Dad.

"I'll tell you in a minute," he said.

We sat at the back. Ren's gran made Ren and Petie squash up together so they would all three fit on two seats. Ren held her bag tight to her chest. Dad told us that they were going to take turns to do our journeys to school. "We'll do the mornings and Ren's gran has offered to collect you all in her car every day."

Getting a lift home every day by car – that sounded great. I've had some of my best chats in cars.

Chapter 16
Ren

Gran wouldn't let Petie and me just be normal us.

She wanted everything done quietly: *just play quietly, why don't you sit quietly, come down the stairs quietly.* She didn't want us to breathe. She wanted us to be completely gone. She'd rather live with ghosts.

She kept stopping us doing things: We couldn't play in the garden because the plants were too special. So we ended up inside. But there was nothing to do inside. *No screens. You'll ruin your eyesight.*

I ran from the bathroom into the brown spare room. Petie was lying on the floor lining up his cars in their endless traffic jams. I tagged him. "You're it. You've got ten seconds to get me back or you lose."

"That's not fair!"

"It is, too, fair!" And I was off and sprinting down the stairs and across the lounge.

There were so many little wobbly tables with plants and ornaments on little lacy cloths. They made everywhere like an obstacle course.

It wasn't my fault if Petie decided to leap over the table from the doorway without looking. I was already out of the French windows.

Crash!

Gran appeared and shouted at me. "Ren! Come back this minute! Just look what you've made him do."

Petie was staggering to his feet. The table had fallen over and the plant had sprayed soil across the carpet. The broken bits of the lady on the swing ornament were scattered across the floor. She must have been on the little table.

I looked at the floor. "I didn't *make* him do *anything*," I said.

Gran stood panting in the doorway. Her apron said *Her Ladyship*. She folded her arms. "I will not have you answering back under my roof," she snapped.

"But you asked me about it."

Her face was like thunder. She bent to pick up bits of the lady. "Must I remove all my lovely things before you smash the rest of them?" she said.

"It wasn't me," I said. "But … sorry."

She bit her lips together. "Petie looks to you, Ren. The idea came from you."

"But we were only chasing."

"In my house."

She always said about it being *her* house. *We haven't got a house,* I wanted to shout back. *This is the only one we can be in, you old dragon!* But I didn't say that. I said, "There isn't anywhere else."

"You've had a whole day at school. Do your chasing there."

Gran moved the little tables and ornaments upstairs into her room. She even dragged a rug up there. I didn't know whether I should offer to help. She would probably think I'd smash something. So I didn't.

Where did she want us to play, on the roof? The house filled with her angry mood until Mum came in, heard what we did and told us off as well. Mum was really cross about the broken ornament. "We'll replace it, of course, Stella."

"I don't think that's possible. I bought it some years ago. I've moved some of my precious items upstairs," Gran said.

"Of course. Of course."

Mum had a furious face. "You have to treat Gran's house with care," she told us. "You never used to be like this."

"It's because everything wobbles," Petie said. "The table…"

"I'm not interested in the table," Mum said. "This is someone else's house. You're like a couple of wild things. I'm ashamed of you."

I escaped upstairs and found myself outside Gran's room. I wanted to see the little cupboard again. What were the things that had sparkled?

I glanced back along the corridor, my fingers reaching for the door. Gran appeared at the top of the stairs. "Don't hang around there, Ren," she said.

I had to edge back past her, making myself thin. I felt her angry eyes on me as I slid inside the brown spare room. I stuck my tongue out a tiny bit when she couldn't see.

Petie and me lay on our beds and growled at each other.

"You are a poo."

"No, you are a poo."

*

Later, at dinnertime, there was a frosty feeling and we sat looking down in our laps, wishing for the meal to be over so we could get back upstairs. Gran said, "I see no reason why you couldn't help more, Ren. Don't you usually help at home?"

I shrugged.

"Well, you're old enough to offer. Where do you think meals come from?"

I didn't want to answer back again so I just stayed quiet. "I'm waiting for an answer, Ren," she snapped.

If I spoke, that was answering back. If I didn't answer, that was rude. It didn't make any difference what I said. I was the worst person.

It wasn't just us who were prickly. Maybe it was mostly *her*.

After dinner I wandered into the garden and stood outside the caravan. Why were Mum and Dad never there to play with us any more? Why were they always working?

The window was a little bit open, and I could hear them talking in there even though there was a printer whirring right by the window. I got ready to knock so they wouldn't be cross about me bursting in.

Dad asked Mum something.

Mum replied and I caught some words: *We can't lose the house…*

I couldn't hear what Dad said next and anyway I had stepped back and lowered my hand. How could you *lose* a house? Our house was crumbled down from all the fire damage but … even if our house wasn't properly there, we knew the address. They were going to build it again.

I stood there puzzling … you might lose a shoe or an earring. You put it somewhere and forget where. But how could someone *lose* a house? Had Mum really said that? Could I have heard a different word? Could she have said *choose the house*?

I stood on the path and kicked at the gravel with my trainer. That word wouldn't fit either. Choose it for what?

It was definitely *lose* that Mum said. And she'd sounded so worried.

Chapter 17
Ren

It had been six days since the fire and I was still wondering what things we would get back. One little animal from my collections would be great. I crossed my fingers sometimes when I thought about it. My silver elephant would be good. He had a red enamelled saddle to give rides. He was one of the first things I ever collected.

Mum came into the kitchen carrying a box. She sighed. "I said not to get your hopes up, Ren, love. There's nothing of yours."

"Is there more to come?"

"No, love, this is all of it."

She was holding our family biscuit tin, the rectangular one that always sat on our kitchen table. "There's a few things the fireman found that we might want to look through." She tipped out the contents: small things from the kitchen drawers that weren't ruined – keys and clips and cutlery.

I had always loved our biscuit tin. It was red, orange and yellow and had *Family Selection* in big round letters moulded into the metal. Dad told me that when I was really small I used to bang it with a wooden spoon.

On the lid was a picture of a circus scene: jumping people doing flips and cartwheels. The clever thing was that all the stunts had biscuits in them somehow, performers juggling and throwing them in the air, dancers, clowns and gymnasts with biscuit hoops. There were even prancing horses with biscuit-wheel carriages and a man being shot from a cannon in a shower of biscuits. I used to imagine the contortionist with bendy legs wrapped round his head and try to copy him on the carpet.

Petie and me had biscuits with a drink after school. We used to argue in the supermarket about which packets to buy. Custard creams, jam sandwiches, raisin ones and chocolate chip. Mum would let us choose a packet each and empty them into the tin when we got home from the shops.

Now our family tin had turned dark grey and the circus acts had turned to ghosts; you could only just make out their smoky outlines on the metal.

I looked carefully at the tin sitting on Gran's smart blue tablecloth. It looked all wrong there, black and ghostly, its lid warped and twisted. I ran my fingers over the metal; what had been smooth was now gravelly and pitted with little holes, like lava when it's set. The world of the circus had turned to a place of smoke. The big top had gone. The jolly performers had all blended and melted together, changing into a squashed-together squidge with no background.

"We can't have *that* on the table here," Petie said. "It will make us too sad. It's only a shadowbox now."

A Shadowbox.

Petie was right. No one would ever put biscuits in our tin – they would smell of smoke and go soft because the lid didn't fit.

"I don't think the firemen meant us to have the tin back. They were just looking for something to put the little things from the drawer in," Mum said, not looking up.

But I wanted the tin. It reminded me of our cheery kitchen. You could still see the circus if you looked hard.

Mum threw the tin in Gran's recycling with the bent lid squashed down the side of the crate.

That evening I fished it out and hid it upstairs in Dad's old university trunk.

I didn't actually have a plan for the tin. I just didn't want it to be gone. But later a plan sort of … arrived.

Chapter 18
Ren

Gran seemed pleased about the new arrangement with Caspar's dad. She explained that he would take us to school with Caspar on the bus every day and she would pick us up in the car at the end of school. "Better for all of us," she said. "I can do one or two more of my normal activities." When she smiled, Gran looked different. Not better. She had the wrong face for smiling.

I didn't know Caspar, even though we were in the same class. He sat at the desks at the front, near the reading corner. I knew he was annoying, though. In school he was always calling out suggestions. He asked more questions than anyone I had ever met, even teachers.

I decided Gran taking us to school and picking us up was worse because Gran was like an army sergeant, expecting us by the door at exactly eight fifteen and listening to weird classical music in the car. *No interruptions, please.* I would just have to put up with Caspar's nosy questions.

Caspar and his dad were more relaxed, messing around at the bus stop, pointing out unusual things from the bus. The first day Petie and me travelled with him, Caspar said to me, "Do you ever go back and visit your house? Did they find things? I mean, metal things wouldn't burn so much … maybe … a washing machine?"

"A lot of the house fell down. The rest got knocked down and taken away in skips because it was just rubble," I said. I turned away and looked out of the window as the streets flashed by. Most people get it that you don't want to talk any more if you stare out of the window. Not Caspar.

"So will you get a new house?"

"They're trying to sort it out." I said. And then some words came into my head and I just said them. "They're worried about *losing it*," I told him.

Caspar nodded. "Oh … do you think they might? Have your mum and dad got a *mortgage* or were they renting it?"

A mortgage? I didn't know this word. It seemed to be an important one. Caspar seemed to know all about houses. "I don't know," I said. "It was just … our house."

I hadn't told anyone about Mum's *losing it* comment, but Caspar looked interested. Maybe he could explain. Mum and Dad might get really upset if I asked them about a mortgage. I didn't want to make them feel worse!

I turned to face him. "What's a mortgage?"

"Well, it's clever. My brother explained it to me because he's renting, which means you pay money to the person who owns the house or flat or whatever it is but *you* never own it. But a person with a mortgage is borrowing the money from a bank. They keep paying for a house, while they live in it, and then one day, when they've paid loads of money for years and years, the bank say, you've paid enough now, it's yours."

Something fell away inside me. "So if you're living in it and still supposed to be paying the mortgage … you could still … *lose it* if you couldn't pay?"

Caspar nodded. "Well, I think you could, yes."

I stared out of the bus window again. My thoughts were grim. What Caspar had said made Mum's comment make sense. "Who gets the house … if you lose it? If you can't pay?" I said in a normal kind of voice.

Caspar seemed to think. "Well … I think the bank gets it."

"Oh."

Now something inside me came crashing down. No wonder Mum and Dad were so worried. No wonder they practically lived in the caravan the whole time and hardly ever came to talk to us or play or watch TV.

The losing-the-house thoughts swirled around in my head, like poisoned water in a well.

Caspar was pointing out of the window at a dog. "See that dog down there. That's like my dog, Snaffle." He turned to me, still with a smiling face. "At least your grandma's house is in the same town. Is it like … being on holiday?"

I felt cross with him now. "No," I said, putting him straight. "Because holidays are fun."

Chapter 19
Ren

I went to Amelia's for tea. "I have to find some clothes to go in my box for the project," she said. "It has to be *something you like to wear*. I am *so* stuck!"

I sat on her bed beside a heap of clothes as more and more things poured out of her wardrobe.

I was stuck too, but not like Amelia was stuck. I was stuck because I didn't have anything I liked to wear any more. I only had our neighbour Alice's clothes and some emergency things Mum bought from the supermarket while I was at school. Alice's clothes were nicer styles but they were too big for me and some looked old and a bit stretched.

The mirror opposite me was from Amelia's holiday and the edge was made up of tiny chips of pottery and glass. Close up the chips looked random, but they weren't. It was a mosaic. When you were close, there were broken-up colours but when you stood back from it the picture was of the countryside and animals and people working in a field. I moved near and then away, trying to find the place where the picture would become clear. Imagine if all the small things I used to own were laid close to each other, each one just a colour or a shape, but when you stood back from it they made me – a picture of me.

Amelia paraded around the room, inspecting different hoodies and tops. "Gross!" she said, and then, holding up a stripy jumper, "I've always liked this one!"

The two of us used to go clothes shopping together on a Saturday so I recognised loads of the clothes. There was a hoodie with rainbows and the sun in the pile. I remembered choosing a dark-blue one the same sort with stars on.

"This is boring. Let's try them all on!" Amelia handed the jumper to me. "You try some too. I won't know until I see them on."

When Amelia suggests something, it's easier if you just say yes. It wasn't too bad trying on her clothes. It felt like the old Amelia and me. And anyway, we're the same size. We made a pile of things we'd tried and she shouted marks out of ten to help her choose a winner. "Hideous! That is a total two!" Her top picks went in a heap on the bed ready for her final choices.

She was in the loo when I saw the sun top low down on her wardrobe shelf. In a flash I was back all those months ago in June, in a small shop near the arcade. I took it off the shelf and tried it on, fastening up the small pearly buttons. We had bought one each. It was the only piece of clothing that we both owned. It was so bright, made up of panels of red and blue geometric patterns like a quilt. It had beading round the neckline. I remembered persuading Amelia to buy one because I loved it so much. "We can be twins!" My one had faded a bit because I'd worn it all summer. Of course, now mine was gone anyway.

I stood staring at old me in Amelia's full-length mirror. The sun top wasn't on Amelia's top-picks pile. It hadn't even made it into her *possibles*. It was me who had loved it. Amelia was always extravagant about clothes and her mum let her spend loads of money. I gazed at the sun top and I wanted it so badly an ache started deep down in my stomach. My fingers began to tingle. All at once I was pulling my school shirt on over the top, fingers flying, scrabbling to do up the buttons, then cramming my sweatshirt over my head.

My heart pounded as if I'd run a race.

I walked to the window and looked out at the garden. When I pressed through my shirt below the collar I could feel the bumps of the beads inside my clothes.

I felt hot. My skin prickled.

So … I might have kept on Amelia's sun top by mistake, like I'd forgotten I was wearing it. It was a really comfy design, like a vest. Yes, it could have been just a mistake.

Probably she wouldn't mind anyway, even if she knew. Maybe she would have given me the top if I'd asked her. In a way the sun top could be a shared thing. Maybe it was like getting my own one back and we would sort of both have it.

A few seconds later Amelia came racing back and we laughed about which of the hoodies and tops she should choose for her box all over again.

Nothing bad happened. Amelia was fine… Fine.

I put the sun top in the Shadowbox when I got home.

Dad's old university trunk was a good place to hide it. I had heard Gran asking him to clear it out. There were so many bags inside, books and shoes as well as games and toys. I knew Dad wouldn't get round to it any time soon; he was far too busy. And with the plant and the cloth on top my box was safe. Definitely safe.

Chapter 20
Ren

Dad came in to eat tea with us that evening. In Gran's house Dad seemed different. He told Petie, "Don't slurp your water." Dad never normally said things like that.

Petie looked amazed. His eyes filled with tears.

We all ate our sausages without looking at each other, trying to be elegant. Dad seemed to be watching me as much as Gran did. My elbows stuck out. I pulled them in and cut smaller and smaller bits of sausage.

Dad waved his fork towards the green pile of vegetables on the side of my plate. "Eat up your broccoli," he said.

Gran dabbed at her mouth with the napkin as if she was injured. "It's kale," she said.

Dad nodded. "Of course, kale."

"I hate kale, Dad," Petie said.

We all looked at Gran. She got up and went through to the kitchen to refill the water jug.

"I would eat peas. She never gives us peas," Petie said sadly.

Dad shovelled Petie's kale on to his own plate, plunged in his fork and took a big mouthful.

"I don't want the kale either," I said.

"You're older," Dad said, chomping on green bits.

"I still hate it."

"Try," he said.

Dad went to the loo. Now both of them were gone, I shovelled my kale on to Gran's plate, leaving one tiny bit that I ate.

Petie's mouth opened wide. "Ooh, Ren, I'm telling."

"Don't you dare!"

I shouldn't have said that. Petie's eyes were gleaming.

When Dad and Gran came back, Petie kept giggling while we all sat there eating again. I kicked him under the table.

Gran looked up. Her lips went tight and she paused with a forkful of food near her mouth.

Petie exploded in giggles.

"What's the big joke?" Dad said.

"Ask Ren," Petie snorted.

"What's going on?" Dad asked.

I shrugged. "No idea, Dad." I glared at Petie.

"Ren did a thing…"

"Now, I'll not have telling tales," Gran said. She loaded a big pile of green stuff on to her fork. Petie was lost in another burst of giggles.

Gran turned her head away with a sniff. "How are things going?" she asked Dad. "Any news?"

Dad sighed. "Rachel's badgering them to sort out the claim. We've just got so much to do. Your help with the kids is just brilliant, Mum."

I think Petie would still have told but then he knocked over his glass of water and Dad and Gran ended up mopping it up.

I wished we had Mum. Mum would understand about the food. The sort of work Mum and Dad did needed *headspace*, Mum would often tell me before the fire. Now, though, Mum and Dad never seemed to be with us together. It was as if they had shared us out, like another job.

Mum still came to say goodnight to us, though.

She hugged Petie first. "We must get you both some books," she said. Then she came over to my bed and lay down beside me. "How are things?" she asked. Her voice was a *sorting-out* voice. Old Mum would have laughed about the food and getting Gran to eat my green stuff but I didn't tell her. She kissed me and gave me a hug.

"Things are … OK," I said.

"Great," she whispered, and began to pull away. Usually she stayed longer but nowadays I didn't think she had any headspace left with all the worries. I didn't want her to go. "Are *you* OK, Mum?" I asked in the dark.

Her arms went round me again, wrapping me close. "We're drowning a bit, but we're doing our best. Get to sleep, love."

"Goodnight, Mum," I said, letting her go.

But once she was gone, I thought, *What did that mean?* What had Mum meant about *drowning*? I had wanted to understand the losing-the-house conversation but now a new word filled the room. Now Mum and Dad were *drowning*!

Chapter 21
Caspar

When Jake was sketching faces to show us how to do self-portraits, I noticed his pen. It was a cool fountain pen that filled with ink from a bottle. It was a deep-blue colour with swirls and reminded me of the sea. The ink he was using was purple. I hadn't watched someone use a fountain pen to draw before and he did long sweeps.

"I love this pen," Jake said when I asked him about it. "I think sometimes you do your best work if you have a pen you like to inspire you."

I wanted to take a closer look at Jake's pen, but Miss Chatto said we must get on with the portraits and Jake said, "Another time, bud." When he says no, he says it in a way that doesn't crush you. I really like that about Jake.

Later on we were passing round colouring pencils in a big box. We were allowed to take a selection for our table and I saw Jake's fountain pen in there with the pencils, right up at one end. I thought, *Oh, whoops, that shouldn't be in the box*. But Theo grabbed a handful of pencils and passed the box to the next table. I thought no one would take Jake's pen out. It would just circulate and get back to him. We were all working feverishly on our portraits and I was trying very hard to make the eyes work on mine (they were actually getting worse, not better – they looked as if they were sliding down the face). Anyway, Jake called out, "Has anyone seen my fountain pen, the one I was using earlier?" And I said, "Well, in fact, yes, it came round in the pencil box."

Miss Chatto looked puzzled and dug around among the pencils. "Are you sure, Caspar?"

Everyone looked at me.

Was I sure? Hadn't anyone else seen it in the box? I felt a bit wobbly. Surely someone would call out, "Here, I've got it!"

I waited. It didn't happen; everyone else looked blank. My memory is good but I wondered if maybe I'd been wrong. Maybe Jake's pen hadn't been passed round and I'd seen some kind of special pencil that looked a bit like it.

"Let me think," I said.

"Did you see Jake's pen or didn't you?" Miss Chatto asked. "It's a valuable pen."

Valuable! Oh no! "Oh goodness," I said. "Yes. I still think I did. I'm about seventy-five per cent sure."

"So why didn't you tell us?" She actually sounded a bit cross.

I felt even more wobbly. Jake was staring at me with that wide friendly look, but he was also digging, searching all over the desk.

I breathed a big gulp of air. "I'm sorry I didn't say and I don't know why I didn't take the pen out of the box."

Everyone stared at me as if I was definitely *unreliable*.

"Could you all have a look around your desks, please?" Miss Chatto said.

The whole class began crawling and wandering about and banging desk lids. I got down on the floor and searched under my desk, round the back of the chairs and all the way to the radiator.

"It'll turn up," Jake said.

But by the end of the afternoon his pen hadn't turned up. I kept noticing Miss Chatto muttering things and looking over at me with a puzzled frown. I went over in my mind the order of the people who'd had the pencil box because I had another thought; what if someone took Jake's pen *deliberately* just after I passed the box round? Who had Theo passed the box to next? If it had gone round most of the class, then more people would have seen it. Theo said he gave it to the window table. Who? He wasn't sure. I wanted to say all this to Miss Chatto but then I'd be accusing someone, wouldn't I?

No one found Jake's pen. I wondered who the next pair of hands had been. Someone on the window table. They were all looking down, busy with their drawings. I even doubted myself and tipped out my backpack on the desk just in case the pen had dropped into it, but it wasn't there.

Someone else must have it. They must.

When I got home, I got into a complicated

discussion with Mum when I tried to explain because somehow it felt a bit like it was my fault, like I'd let Jake down. Mum said the pen would turn up, but it wasn't found and I was connected to it disappearing. So the next day I kept checking around the classroom. People got fed up with me asking them. Miss Chatto talked about not bringing valuable things into school. She didn't exactly say it but we must have a thief in our class. It was a horrible thought, but we must.

Chapter 22
Ren

The fountain pen was in the box of pencils that came round the classroom when we were making our self-portraits, a beautiful blue one. My fingers began to tingle. I picked out that pen along with two pencils. I looked around. Everyone was chatting and drawing. I moved the pen to my lap and turned it over and over.

Everyone was saying how hard it is to draw yourself. "Mine is nothing like me!" people called and laughed. The portraits had massive noses and googly eyes. Jake kept saying, "Think about your head shape. If you get that right, it's much easier to make the eyes and nose look right. Remember the ones we looked at in the art gallery."

I had missed that trip. I hadn't seen any of those portraits he kept going on about.

I could feel the weight of the pen in my lap. Maybe Jake had meant to pass that pen round for us to use. I love fountain pens. This one was smooth and blue with a shiny pattern like a polished stone. I wriggled my legs and it shifted around on my lap. Think of all the drawing this pen could do. I like when a thing is a one-off. Before the fire, I had a fountain pen among my art materials that was my grandad's. It was dark brown, like a chestnut. Having a fountain pen meant you took care with writing and drawing.

"If you work hard on the eyes, it's like getting closer to the real you," Jake said.

We shouldn't be doing this project. A big rush of feelings washed around inside me. Why were they forcing us to do this stupid *box of me* project? It was making everything worse. All those things I was meant to collect that made me who I was. And Jake – well, it was all his fault, wasn't it? I hated him for making us do this. *And* he didn't care that I missed the art gallery. My blood seethed.

Adults kept saying, "Oh, Ren, we're sorry if this is hard for you."

They didn't understand.

I drew me transformed to a witch with the wildest hair. I went on drawing my wild-hair witch even when everyone else was messing about and pretending to look for the pen. I drew green tangles. I drew red squiggles radiating out from a smouldering face.

When we gave the pencils back, I dropped the pen in my book bag and shut it. Serve him right.

When I got home, I put the pen with the sun top in the Shadowbox inside Dad's trunk and put back the plant and the cloth on top.

✗

After that day something switched in me. My eyes had turned to secret laser lamps. Every day I looked for *things*.

My body had an ache; not a headache or a tummy ache – an all-of-me ache.

My fingers bracing … tingling… My eyes checking around me.

I was good at this.

Anything could be happening: noise and rushing, but I felt as if I was inside a silent space, like a bubble.

Countdown: Ten … nine … eight…

Nearer.

Eye dart. Seven, six, five…

Nearly mine.

Four … three … two… Groping out … closing in.

One.

Mine.

Mishe wouldn't notice the neon highlighter was gone. She would just buy more of them and probably a nicer blue one to replace this one as it was a bit scuffed round the top. Maybe I'd helped her and now she'd get a better one faster.

That sharpener under Ayra's table wasn't named. It looked like the Eiffel Tower. It was broken. I mended the clip that attached it to the keyring. So, in a way, it was *my* mended keyring.

Sohail's animal ruler was between us on the desk in science. I'm not completely sure it was his. He left it just lying there when he went to lunch. I don't think he cared about it. Maybe he had another one at home.

My Shadowbox was filling up.

Chapter 23
Caspar

It was getting easier to talk to Ren. On the way to school sometimes I sat next to her on the bus but mostly she sat with her brother and I sat with Dad. But in the car on the way home we all squashed into the back. I wouldn't have minded being at the front and talking to Ren's grandma, but on the first day she said, "Right, all of you, climb in the back sensibly." Ren and Petie fought for the two window sides so I often ended up in the middle. Well, always, in fact. Being with them was a loud environment. *That's mine. I was first. Stop elbowing me.*

"You two are like a zoo," I said one time.

"Then I'm a lion!" Petie said.

"You are so not a lion," Ren said.

I laughed. "You're arguing again!"

I actually think it was a good thing I was there.

✗

A new pattern started. I would go back to Ren's grandma's house each day for a while and play with Ren and Petie and then I would walk home a bit later on. Mum and Dad said yes, OK, fine when I suggested it. "If that's what you'd like."

"It makes more sense for me to come and be with you," I told Ren's grandma. "Plus, I could polish some things."

She smiled. "I'm not sure there are many things to polish but … come anyway. As long as you all play quietly."

Sometimes both Mum and Dad had late meetings. Soon after the lifts started Ren's grandma agreed with Dad that I should stay for tea as well on those evenings.

The first time I stayed, in the car I said, "How was everyone's day?" but it got lost in the traffic noise on the one-way system and Ren and Petie arguing.

Once we got to the house, I finished my homework before tea and then offered to lay the table. Ren's grandma said, "Very kind."

Tea was very different from being at home but there was a good smell coming from the kitchen. Ren's grandma said, "Wash hands, three, two, one, table."

We all had white napkins that were really small cloths with a leaf print.

Ren and Petie poked the stew. "What's this?"

"Those are butterbeans, with the pork," their grandma said.

I scooped a big mouthful. It coated my teeth. "Mmm, this is delicious," I said.

"No it isn't; it's yuck," Ren said.

"I can't eat this," Petie wailed.

I laughed.

Ren's grandma threw down the spoon and we all jumped. "This is ridiculous," she muttered.

We all sat a bit frozen, so I said, "In my house we eat the same meals over and over. This is much better than some of our meals actually."

I pulled a basket of bread towards me while everyone watched. "Look, if you dip bread in it, you can eat the sauce and pretend it's a kind of sandwich." I ripped apart some bread to show them. "Try it." I soaked the bread in the sauce and crammed it in my mouth. "It's great," I tried to say but the words got tangled in bread and my mouth was too full. *Pop!* A big wet chunk flew across the table and rolled along the white cloth making an orange trail.

We all stared at it.

"In my house my dog would have got to that by now," I said.

Ren's grandma made a little gulpy noise in her throat. She wrapped her hand in a napkin like a bandage and picked up the bit of spat-out bread. Then she dabbed the orange wet stain with the napkin.

I wondered if I should ask for the bit of bread back. "In my house—"

"Shall we all just eat our food in silence now? We're not in your house, are we?"

I nodded. It was a great meal. We were all quiet again and I got busy eating. The stew was so good. It warmed me up. At home we all eat fast. My plate was nearly empty now. "How will you get that orange mark out of the cloth?" I asked.

"Soak it." Ren's grandma's voice was flat.

"Ren said you used to be a head teacher?" I said.

"Yes."

"So you were in charge of a whole school?"

"I was, yes."

"Did you like it and also was it near here and also do you still see the children you used to teach?"

Ren's grandma shook her head and smiled at the same time. "Which question do you want me to answer?"

"Well, probably that last one. I mean, it doesn't really matter where the school was."

"Have you thought of asking just one question, Caspar?"

I smiled back. "You're right. I just … get interested."

"I can see that." She stopped piling the plates. "I do see the children I used to teach sometimes. They have families of their own now."

"Really! Now that is … well, that is really … amazing."

"Is it?"

"Well, yes, I mean, do they say hello?"

"Some do."

"They must be remembering all the funny things that happened."

Ren and Petie sat eating all the bread dipped in the sauce.

"Can I have Ren's butterbeans?" I asked, because I could see they were just going to go to waste.

I shovelled a big forkful and sloshed pureed beans around my mouth. "I love butterbeans. It's weird, though; they don't seem to have anything to do with butter."

Ren's grandma smiled. "You're a bit of a vacuum cleaner, aren't you, Caspar?"

"You should meet my brother. In my house you have to be quick. If I go to the loo, Matty just takes my bacon. You have to eat fast. And Snaffle is such a thief. He's like a bottomless pit. He's by the table, sniffing all the smells. Did you know that dogs have ten thousand times the smelling ability of humans? He's a golden retriever. He's crazy but we all love him."

"Is he yours?" Petie asked.

"We all share him," I said. "He's too big for just one owner. It's a funny name. It's because he snaffles food. He knows it's not his and he sneaks up when no one's looking and just snaps it up. He can't help himself. So we always say, 'Stop it, Snaffle. Put that down. It's not yours.' And he's got this look on his face like *Please, please can I have it?* Or sometimes he gives you a look that says *What, me? I don't know what you're talking about!* He's cheeky like that. Soon as your back is turned, he's there."

"Do you take him for walks?" Petie asked.

I laughed. "No, he takes me!"

Petie sat up very straight. "Could you bring him ... here, please?"

I couldn't imagine Snaffle in here. He would crash around. He wouldn't mean to but he would mess everything up and maybe even break things.

Petie's grandma clattered the plates. "Maybe ... you could join Caspar on a walk," she said. "If the weather was reasonable and you had an adult with you."

"Of course you can," I said.

Chapter 24
Ren

Our teacher, Miss Chatto, was really nice. I liked her long fingers and her small mouth. Her neat eyebrows were like the caterpillars we found on the moors once on holiday. She was neat in every way. I liked the way she lined things up on the desk, arranging her pencils from shortest to longest.

Miss Chatto smiled at us a lot. Her long hair was swept back off her face and clipped behind her head. She played with hairclips when she was teaching us. She unclipped the clip and worked the spring between her fingers, sometimes trapping her fingers in the gripper bit, which must hurt. Other times she trapped the top edge of the hole punch in the gripper or some sheets of paper. It was like her plaything. The clips were very beautiful and all different. Some were shaped like birds. I think maybe she chose a clip every day to match her clothes.

One lunchtime, when I was on my own in the classroom, I noticed Miss Chatto's hairclip on the floor under her desk. It was her usual claw type. *Oh, wow.* I moved nearer, checking no one was about. I stared at the clip. It was made of a heavy metal, as big as my hand with smart gripper hooks. It was one of her most beautiful ones decorated with clouds in blue and purple on a pale-blue sky.

It could easily get broken down there. It could be smashed completely if someone wasn't looking and their big shoe crushed it.

My fingers started tingling. My laser eyes darted to left and right.

Where?

Up my sleeve, then in my coat in the cloakroom?

I studied the shape. My heart pumped hard. It would make a big lump in my sleeve.

Think. My eyes scanned the room. My lunch box was nearby on my desk. *Perfect. Yes, then straight to the cloakroom.* I grabbed my lunch box and eased off its lid.

Blood pounded in my head. One more glance towards the door.

My hand closed round the claw, grasped it. It felt heavier than I had expected. I dropped it in my lunch box and rammed the lid back on.

The door banged and I spun round. Amelia was standing there. "Why are you always inside, Renee?"

"I was just finishing my lunch."

She glanced at the lunch box in my hand. "Got any food left?"

My heart hammered. I didn't want to swing the lunch box because the claw would clatter inside it. "No. Gran gave me a disgusting fish sandwich today," I said, holding it still.

Amelia gripped her nose. "Poo, gross! Your gran's lunches are soooo horrible!" She reached to grab my arm and I swapped the lunch box into my other hand and did a wild high-five wave with the other one.

Must get to the cloakroom. I smiled and strolled towards the door. "I'll just put my lunch box in my bag. I'll be out in a sec."

Amelia was gone, slamming the outside door behind her.

In the cloakroom among the coats, I held on to the hooks for a moment, breathing out. Next minute, I was pulling off the padding of my shocking-pink earmuff and pushing Miss Chatto's clip inside it. Now, that was a clever idea!

In afternoon registration Miss Chatto moved things around on her desk, gathering up piles of our writing books and balancing some pots of pens on a chair.

"Have you lost something, miss?" Ellie asked.

"I don't know." Miss Chatto pushed her hair back off her face. "Maybe. Have any of you seen my hairclip?"

There was a murmur. "No, miss. Sorry, miss."

"Shall we all look for it?" asked Caspar. "We could all crawl around on the floor. I think it would be good for everyone to have a break."

Some people moved their chairs and talking broke out.

Miss Chatto smiled and put up her hand for quiet. "That's a kind idea, Caspar, but I've probably left my clip at home. I'm not certain I even wore it today."

Then my voice. "Your clip could have fallen in the recycling, miss. I could look through the bin for it in afternoon play, if you want?"

Everyone stared over at me. Miss Chatto smiled. "How very kind, Ren," she said.

I spent the whole of afternoon play searching. It was strange but I really felt like I might find the claw, like it could somehow be magically back.

Miss Chatto came back from the staffroom with her tea in her travel mug. She sighed. "Thanks, honey. Never mind. Keep a lookout."

I smiled at her. "I'm sure it'll turn up."

✗

At home I cradled the hairclip. I pinched the gripper. Lots of hairclips are plastic but this one was a plate of enamel colours on silvery metal. I stroked it. I pushed the top sections to make it grab my finger. "Ow!" I said softly.

Later, when I'd opened the Shadowbox, I nestled it beside the pen in the folds of the sun top, and closed the material gently round it. I felt closer to Miss Chatto now. And I had saved the clip from being broken. I was a rescuer.

I went outside and peeped inside the caravan but Mum and Dad were both bent over their desks, probably talking to the bank or trying to get the contract ready.

I went back upstairs and wandered along the landing to Gran's room.

There was a key in the lock. I hadn't noticed that before.

Gran came out. "Is everything all right?" she asked, blocking the doorway.

I nodded.

"Good … good," she said.

I retreated back to the brown spare room.

I told Petie all sorts of things that might be in Gran's room. He kept asking and I kept adding more. Maybe she had puppets hanging up of children she had got angry with when she was a head teacher. Imagine her in charge of a whole school, I told him. Maybe there were super-soakers in there ready to blast naughty children messing about under her window. Or a revolting eyeball that could jump out and whop you. Or a pan for boiling children in. That's why she kept a room for no one else to see. *Watch out*, I told him, *because she will drag you in there.*

✗

That night Petie wet the bed. He poked me awake

and told me. "Don't go in Gran's room, Ren," he said. "You'll never get out." He got in my bed and I found him clean pyjamas and told him a Mr Softie story about Mr Softie riding a horse. We slept end to end in my bed with his feet by my head. We didn't wake Gran. Next morning, she covered Petie's mattress with a plastic-jacket thing that squeaked. Petie said it made him sore and hot.

If you did something wrong at Gran's, she told you to sit on the stairs. I quite liked sitting on the stairs so it wasn't a real punishment. She didn't punish Petie for the bedwetting. If it had been me, she would've.

Chapter 25
Caspar

More things disappeared from our class.

Miss Chatto called it a "spate of thefts" and she looked very upset. "I can't believe it," she said. "It hurts all of us."

I put my hand up.

She sighed. "What is it, Caspar?"

"Please, miss, what's a 'spate'?"

"A flood," she said.

"Is a spate a bad thing?"

"Not always, but in this case yes," she said, staring at me hard.

Spate's an interesting word. I like using new

words a lot. I decided I would say to Dad that he'd given me a spate of tuna sandwiches. And I would chat to Mum about the spate of Snaffle waking up very early the last few days.

Everyone rushed outside for break. I hummed the word *spate* to myself. Then I noticed Miss Chatto was looking up at me.

"Do you think maybe if you tidied away more of the things on your desk that you might find some of the lost things?" I asked her.

Her mouth fell open. "What do you mean?"

"Well, you are quite messy," I said.

"Caspar, that's not an appropriate thing to say to a teacher."

"Oh, sorry. I'm messy too. We all are at home. My dad's the worst."

"Did you have a question?" Miss Chatto's voice sounded low and just a bit harsh. She looked at me in a cold way. "You seem to prefer being inside the classroom to being in the playground."

"I … I … not always," I said. "I'll go out there now."

I didn't know what to do to help make a nicer atmosphere. I offered to come in at lunchtime, sharpen all the pencils and clear up a bit but Miss

Chatto said no one was allowed in at lunchtime, "absolutely not".

There was an assembly about rules and right and wrong. Mrs Isaac said, "We are a community and we stand or fall on people keeping to these rules." She said, "Some people's things have gone missing and in a community we all have to keep things safe. This is a very serious matter."

Although she talked to the whole school, she was bound to be thinking about our class. "Don't bring valuables to school," she said. "Don't visit the cloakroom without a reason. Always ask to go to the loo and try to go at break or lunchtime. No one should be in their classroom at lunchtime without permission."

Don't visit the cloakroom is a tricky rule because you go through the cloakroom to get to the classrooms, so you can't really avoid it. I wondered if I should ask about that, but if you put your hand up in assemblies everyone looks at you and it makes you feel jittery, even if you are asking a good question. Also, I've noticed that some people are allowed to ask questions and, when other people do it, the teacher makes a face where their eyes roll up, a bit like an eye test.

Not now, Caspar or *Ask me later*, they always say. Sometimes Miss Chatto even does a finger on the lips, meaning *Total silence*. I'm pretty sure she does that towards me more than anyone else.

Dad says if you have a question, it's all about choosing your moment. He says adults get stressed and you need to time your question carefully. So I waited until we were back in class, and then I said to Miss Chatto, "The thing is, Mrs Isaac said we mustn't be in the cloakroom but the cloakroom is like a corridor, so it doesn't really make sense to tell us to avoid it."

Miss Chatto breathed out and looked up at me. Her fingers stopped tapping the keyboard. She nodded. "She means don't linger, Caspar. Nobody needs to linger in the cloakroom. Has my answer cleared that up for you?"

"That's much clearer," I said. I turned back to the class, who were sorting out their bags and sitting down. "We are allowed *in* the cloakroom; they just don't want us to linger when we put our coats away."

"Sit down now, Caspar," Miss Chatto said. "I'll take it from there."

Jake was back in our class again.

We were all working on our boxes, covering them with decorations and pictures from Jake's pile.

I hadn't talked to Jake for a few days.

"When I first met you, I thought you actually looked like a pirate," I told him.

"Did you?" he chuckled. "Pirates steal things, though."

"Oh yeah, no, I didn't mean like a real one. It was the beard and all the hair and the coat and things."

I had a sudden thought. "I didn't mean to be rude. You didn't think I was, did you?"

"Don't worry. I'm not offended, Caspar," he said.

"Oh, good," I said.

Chapter 26
Ren

Petie and me were doing a lot of screaming because he wouldn't stay in his half of the room.

There was always a winner and it was usually me because I had more breath and did a big gulp before I started and Petie used up all his puff really quickly. *Hands over ears – scream the loudest you possibly can.* Scream to break glass. Screams can do that. I watched an opera singer online and she cracked a glass.

At the top of the stairs when I was screaming I sometimes saw Gran downstairs. Then a door would slam. Sometimes Petie took a big gulp and screamed again, which is cheating. Once Gran appeared in the doorway, mouthing something but I couldn't tell what she was saying. I could see Petie's mouth was still open but the scream coming from my mouth was so loud I couldn't hear anything else. Gran went away.

When I was screaming, I felt as if a giant wind was blowing through me. *I can't hear you. Go away! You are a BLOB. You are less than a BLOB. Get out, get out.*

We stood, our hands pressed tight to our ears, screaming, making disgusting faces, tongues out, eyes goggling.

Tonight was a long one.

Gran appeared. She strode smartly down the hall, grabbed Petie by the arm and forced him into the corner. She clapped her hand over his mouth. "Stop!" she shouted right in his face.

I carried on screaming but now it was only me.

Gran stood there panting, glaring at me. "You stop too, Ren!" she shouted, lunging towards me. I leapt from her clutches but my breath was now all gone and all the screams died. The hall was very quiet.

Gran was looking at us, her eyes so wide they

looked as if they might pop out.

Petie was rubbing his arm and sniffing. "Granny, you made Ren the winner."

"What?" she shouted. "What on earth are you talking about?"

Petie turned up a proud chin. "First one to stop screaming loses. You made me lose."

Gran's mouth opened in a wide gasp.

"And you hurt my arm," Petie went on. Red fingerprints were marked on it.

Gran stroked it. "I'm very sorry," she murmured. "Really very sorry."

Petie sniffed. "Ren says you've got a machine for bad children. Do you?"

Gran glared at me. "That's ridiculous!" She breathed hard. "Such a headache! Look here, I can't bear the screaming."

Petie grinned. "Me too."

Gran looked amazed. "What do you mean?"

"I hate it too but we have to do it," Petie said.

"Why?"

Petie sighed. "Because otherwise we won't know who the winner is."

Gran held on to the banister. "Now, listen here, both of you. You will not do the screaming any more. Do you understand?"

Petie was nodding.

"And you, Ren!"

I squidged my mouth into a very small sideways yes.

"My house, my rules. No more screaming. Is that clear?"

She must have told Dad. Later on he came and found us and said, "I gather you've both been screaming for no reason."

"Not for no reason," I said.

"Well, whatever the reason is, your gran doesn't want screaming and neither do I," Dad said. "So it stops. It is incredibly kind of Gran to have us here."

It's not like the screaming was major fun or anything. It's just … she was always making rules. Gran was a rule machine.

Chapter 27
Caspar

Matty sent a message to say he was coming home for the weekend. *That way I get to see my favourite brother and get spoiled with good food!*

I was so excited. I thought of all the things we'd do. And, ready for his arrival, I put a banner on the door saying *Welcome home, Matty*, covered in stars and flags.

Snaffle had nearly forgotten who Matty was even though he had only been gone six weeks. Maybe because his hair was longer than it had ever been.

Matty brought me a remote-controlled car. It

was a jeep with huge tyres. When you pressed to accelerate, it sped off incredibly fast. I thought I might burst. "This is amazing, Matty. This is—"

"Come on, Pipsqueak," he said. "Let's make some ramps for it."

We made slopes from old bookshelves in the shed and took it out on to the pavement. You could run the jeep towards them and it would leap off and literally fly for a few milliseconds then zoom down the other slope. Snaffle went wild, yapping at it, thinking it was an enemy out to get him.

"This is brilliant!" I told Matty as we made the jeep jump off the ramp over and over. My brother smiled. He was texting someone on his phone.

"How about we make a second ramp or a bridge?" I called, running inside the shed to search for more stuff.

When I came out, Matty had disappeared.

I ran back inside the house and called him. Matty's head appeared above the banisters. "I'm on a call, Caspar," he said.

I waited for him to come back out. I waited ages. In the end I picked up the jeep and walked back in the house. I could hear Matty on the phone upstairs laughing, going, "Yes you did!"

I went upstairs and tapped on his door. It swung open. "When are you coming back outside?" I asked.

Matty said, "Just a sec," into his phone, then he said, "Caspar, I need to speak to my friends." He ran his hands through his long hair. "I'm, er, going out in ten minutes anyway."

"Can I come?"

"No. I'm meeting somebody. It's not anyone you know."

"But I could get to know them. If you take me. I can't know them if you don't take me."

He shook his head. "You're not coming."

"But…"

"Look, I'll be back later." He grinned at me. "We've got the whole weekend."

"But it'll be dark later. We can't make more ramps outside later."

"Well, we'll make some tomorrow then."

"But tomorrow is hours away."

"Ask one of your friends." His voice was shirty now. "I'm on the phone." He shut the door.

I stared at the door. Matty always included me in everything. He liked my ideas. I gulped and choked. He didn't want me any more.

I went downstairs and found Dad working on his laptop in the kitchen. He pulled me over and ruffled my hair. "How's it going, Caspar?"

"Matty won't play with the jeep on the ramps we made. He doesn't think I'm interesting." I gulped. "He'd rather talk to friends on his phone. And I made him a banner and everything."

Dad hugged me tight. "Caspar, Matty's really pleased to see you." He squeezed me tight, "but..."

"I'm like ... *a reserve*," I sobbed.

"That's not true." Dad sat me down. "Don't be hurt. He needs to meet his college friends. Sometimes he'll be around and sometimes he won't."

"I'm boring."

"Probably you are boring, just a bit, because of the new things he's been doing at uni. Matty doesn't live at home now in term time. His friends are very important. You're important too but ... different."

"But we're his family!"

"He knows that. And he did get you the jeep. He must have thought a lot about you to buy you that."

"Mmm." I had been so excited. Now everything just felt flat.

"Look at me... Give me a hug," Dad said. "Could you ... have some friends over? Why don't you call someone?"

I thought of Ren and Petie. We could have a walk with Snaffle and play with the car.

I rang Ren's grandma because I didn't have Ren's mobile number.

"Hello," said her grandma's voice.

"Good morning, no, afternoon. Would Ren and Petie be free for a dog walk and for tea?"

"You had better speak to Ren," she said.

Then a silence. She must be calling her.

"Hello?" It was Ren.

"It's Caspar. Would you and Petie like to come to my house?"

"When?"

"Actually now."

"Will we meet the dog?" I heard Petie ask in the background.

"Yes," I said. "The dog's included."

They came in just a bit more than half an hour and stayed all afternoon.

Chapter 28
Ren

Dad dropped us off at Caspar's. We waited outside while Caspar found the lead. Snaffle came bounding out and he was so pleased to see us and so excited that we were all laughing. Caspar's dad came for a walk with us. We loved Snaffle the minute we met him. Snaffle was very fluffy and friendly with golden fur and huge eyes. He didn't seem to ever worry about anything. He never stayed still for long and he was off again dragging Caspar up the road with everyone else running behind.

When Snaffle jumped in the air, all his fur whisked high, like feathers. We had to run to keep up with him, but then he would suddenly stop at a tree or a fence and sniff around it as if it was the best smell in the world. We ran and stopped and ran and stopped all the way to the park. Snaffle wanted to smell everything and make friends with every dog he met, leaping and frisking and dragging Caspar into a tangle of leads and dogs and legs. "Sit!" Caspar said, and gave him treats for coming to heel. "We have to make him do as he's told."

When he was off the lead in the park, he got rewarded for coming back. "Good dog. Sit." Caspar whistled to him. "Snaffle!" he said in a high and bright voice. "Come on, boy."

Petie kept laughing at everything Snaffle did. He tried to hug him by putting his arms round Snaffle's tummy. He kept wanting to hold the lead, but he got pulled over completely when Snaffle bolted. Caspar was cross then.

When we got back to the house, we played with Caspar's remote-controlled jeep. He and his brother had made ramps for it. We took it in turns to run it over the ramps and built some extra ones with some wood from his shed. Snaffle had to have a person keeping an eye on him the whole time because he got so excited when the jeep came over the ramps and barked at it as if it was a living thing.

When we went in the house, Caspar's mum said, "Hi, everyone, and great to meet you!" There were hanging lamps with lots of coloured glass pieces and huge plants. The sort of carpets Gran would have on the floor, Caspar's mum had on the walls!

Caspar's mum called, "Help yourselves," and disappeared upstairs. Caspar practically made our tea on his own. I watched while he made a tomato sauce to go with some chicken, toasted some bread and put plates out on the table.

"Do your mum and dad just let you cook?" I asked.

He smiled. "I learned a lot from my brother. He makes great tacos," he said.

We made buns and put toppings on them. Petie sat munching the toppings. At Gran's we would never do that.

Snaffle stole food at teatime. He dragged a bit of chicken off a plate. Petie and me were creased up laughing, but Caspar said, "You mustn't encourage him. Bad dog."

Caspar isn't like a child in his house; he's like an *in-between*. "Where is your brother? I thought he was home for the weekend," I said, while we all sat around on the big floor cushions licking our fingers.

"He is, but he needs to see his friends," Caspar said. "He'll be back later."

When Gran came to collect us, Petie said, "I want to stay here!" and cried.

*

Before bedtime Mum and Dad were both in the kitchen with Gran. Although we got sent to watch telly, their voices drifted through.

"It's not that you're not welcome but … is there still no news on the insurance claim?" Gran said.

I went and stood right by the kitchen door. Were Mum and Dad still drowning?

"Look, we've done everything at our end. The paperwork is all in," said Dad.

"And the contract you're hoping to get?"

"It should all be done in the next couple of weeks. We couldn't have done it without you, Mum."

"Well, it does seem to be taking forever."

"It's quite normal for these kinds of claims. We're on at them every day. There's no point going on about it," Mum said.

"Oh, well, if that's your attitude…" Gran said.

"Calm down!" from Dad.

The voices were rising. They were cross and all

talking at once. Everything felt tangled up and sad.

At Caspar's the grown-ups had laughed. We'd laughed too.

I flopped back on the sofa. I wished I had a Snaffle to cuddle.

Chapter 29
Caspar

Jake's project was a big event every day. People gave talks about their boxes. Eden talked about all the dance performances she does. Her box was full of costumes and programmes from shows she had been in.

My box had a lot of pictures stuck round the inside – equipment for expeditions, information on icebergs. A team of huskies fanned out across the bottom of the box. I'd copied them from a photo.

In our class is a boy called Shabbir. He's been ill but he's getting better. Today he sat at the front of the class to talk about his hobby and his special thing to go in his box and we all sat on tables and chairs in front of him.

"Just plonk yourselves anywhere," Jake said.

When everyone was quiet, Jake said, "So … welcome, Shabbir. Thanks for agreeing to tell us all about your special interest." Jake's eyes twinkled. "Shabbir paints stones, don't you, Shabbir? And today he's going to tell us how he does it."

Shabbir looked up at us. I could see he had something in his hand but his fingers were cupped round it as if it was keeping his hands warm.

"How do you choose which stone to use?" Jake asked.

Shabbir blinked. Three times. "The stones have to be smooth and not too big. The shape … it helps me to have an idea," he said quietly. "I made a frog from a stone that had bumps that looked right for the back legs."

"Great, great!" Jake said. "Have you brought the paints to show us?"

Shabbir emptied the colours on to the desk. There were six tubes. You don't need a big amount," he said. "You squeeze out the colours on a plate."

"Do you draw on the stone first?" Jake asked.

"Yes. I look at the shape and choose if it's a face or a whole animal, like a curled-up cat. I look for especially rounded bits or bits that stick out. Then I draw a sketch and then I paint it."

Shabbir's voice was quite whispery. You could really tell how proud he was of the stones.

"How many stones have you painted so far?" Jake asked.

Shabbir frowned. His lips bit together as he thought. "Five: a mouse – that was my first one and it didn't work very well, a frog, a curled-up cat, a Father Christmas face and this." He opened his hands. Lying in his palm was a ladybird.

"That is amazing!" I said, because the stone was very beautiful.

"Don't all lean forward. We can pass it round," said Miss Chatto.

Shabbir smiled. He doesn't smile very often. "This is my best one," he said.

Every bit of the stone was red with black spots. You could see the shapes of the ladybird's wings and feelers. You felt as if the creature might just crawl away it looked so real. I wished I could make one right then. Mine would be Snaffle's head. Just imagine making a dog's head with lots of paint flecks for its fur.

"Shabbir," Jake said, "how long does each stone take?"

"Maybe … three days." He blinked. "I think I'm getting better at it."

"Well, isn't this fantastic? Big round of applause, guys."

We all clapped.

Shabbir nodded and said something quietly to Jake. "Tell them all that," Jake said. "I love that!"

"It's just … when I hold one of my painted stones in my hand, I feel lucky. They're helping me get better." Shabbir held out the ladybird stone in his palm.

"Lucky stones," Jake said. "I love it!"

Chapter 30
Ren

My fingers were tingling badly today. While everyone was in class, I asked to go to the loo.

There was no one in the cloakroom. My steps slowed. What would I do if someone came by? *Turn towards the peg. Stay perfectly still* … like a hunter. Pretend the coat was mine. Take it off the peg and pretend to search for something in the pocket.

Don't look surprised. Don't look worried. Be slow. Blow your nose, retie a shoe. Never check a thing from a coat. Put it in your pocket and walk on down the corridor. Eyes are giveaways. Look bored.

My fingers tingled like little fireworks going off.

I plunged my hand into a coat pocket, grabbed a small hard plastic thing and swapped it to the pocket of my fleece. My heart was racing. Another coat. Soon I had crowds of things in my pockets: pencils, furry gonks, sweets, tokens, hairclips, rubber bands, toys.

Excitement rushed through me. I felt like I was a bell ringing, full of vibrations. I was so good at this.

Later, in the school library, I noticed a picture book we used to have at home called *Five O'Clock Charlie*. It was the story of a lonely old horse. I flicked through the pictures of the carthorse with his shaggy feet. Petie used to make the sounds for the horse running when Mum and Dad were reading it to us.

Clop-clop, clippety-clop.

I checked inside the book. No one had borrowed it in two years. My fingers tingled. I looked around me. There was no one anywhere nearby. I carried the book out of the library and stuffed it in my school bag when I got to my class.

I was the only one who wanted it. No one else loved *Five O'Clock Charlie*. If they did, they would have borrowed it. It should be mine.

When I sat down, Miss Chatto appeared beside

me. “So, Ren, how are you getting on with the project?” She leaned over me. “Are you finding people to chat to in the class about your ideas? Have you got all the things you need?”

“I don’t know,” I said. “I’ve only just started.”

She smiled. “That’s fine, honey,” she said.

Why didn’t she go and ask someone else? My heart was pounding. *Argh!* My bag with the horse book in was right by her foot. My stuffed pocket was right beside her under the desk. I wanted to put my hand inside and push all the little things deeper down. No. She might look down, see the pocket and wonder why it was so fat.

I wriggled in my chair. *Please move away*, I thought.

“Your mum told me you love to draw. We’ve got some art books. Would you like to copy one or two of the paintings of places or things?”

I nodded, just to make her go away. “OK.”

“Great,” she said. “I’ll bring you some books to look through.”

She stood up and went off to find me the books. *Phew*. She didn’t know my pocket was full of things to draw. And I could have copied some pictures of the horse from the library book. But these were all secret things now.

✗

Back at Gran's I set off upstairs. Mum was at the kitchen table.

Mum and Gran's cross voices chased me up.

"—one bathroom. If people could just think about the towels. Could people PLEASE stick to one towel and hang it up? This morning when I went in—"

"I get it. I'll talk to the kids again. I need to get back to work."

"I haven't finished. While you're doing that, the shoes. There's a perfectly good shoe rack. So why do they just toss the shoes in the general direction of—"

"I've told the kids."

"So tell them again."

"OK, OK!"

"It's not OK!"

On the landing I took the plant off the trunk and pulled it open. I took the Shadowbox out and dropped the new arrivals inside. Leaning over the trunk, I couldn't hear the angry voices any more.

After I put the plant back, I wandered along the landing to Gran's room and tried the door. Locked. Did she lock it every time she came out? Every day? I twisted the knob backwards and forwards. Sometimes in films a person makes a lock picker with a paperclip but I didn't think that would work.

I sank down on the carpet opposite the door. I wondered again about the precious things Gran kept inside her room and the little cupboard in the corner. I pictured it filled with jewels spilling down in a tidal wave, like an Aladdin's cave. I imagined them running through my fingers, bright droplets of rubies and emeralds.

When I had my collections, I used to gently pick up each little glass animal, every shell and painted wooden object and turn them in my hands, feeling the edges, studying the colours before arranging them on a table.

My fingers tingled. Somehow I would get inside Gran's room.

It was like when you're really thirsty, waiting for a drink ... thinking about drinking down that first sip. I was thirsty to be inside that room.

Chapter 31
Caspar

Ellie's water bottle had disappeared. "It was a birthday present," Ellie said. It was gold and shimmery and a famous brand. We searched for it in class but no one had seen it.

"This is unbelievable. When did you last have it?" Miss Chatto asked, sighing.

"Yesterday. Lunchtime, I think. I left it on the windowsill while I was at netball," Ellie said.

Jake was helping to look for the water bottle too. We met in the book corner. "How are you doin', Caspar?" he asked.

"I'm doin' quite good," I said.

"How's the *My Life in a Box* project coming along?"

"Yes. Good. I did more writing for my box at the weekend," I said. "But the problem is I need to finish the edge painting and we don't have any paints like these at home."

Jake grinned. "Is it just one particular colour you need?"

"Well, yes." I picked out the tube of paint from the tray at the back of the room to show him. "Burnt umber … it's sort of brown. But we're not allowed to take the paints home."

"Good colour choice," he said. He beckoned me towards him and dropped his voice. "Take it home with you. Go on. As long as you bring it back tomorrow."

"Oh, can I?"

Jake put his finger to his lips. "Just keep schtum."

"What's 'schtum'?"

"Between ourselves."

"Oh, oh yes. Great. I'll keep schtum then."

"Good lad." He winked and wandered away. I dropped the tube of paint into my school bag. I was glad to be able to work on my box. I would do it tonight. Mum and Dad always seemed to be busy in the evenings at the moment.

The next day, Ren was off school with a bad cold but Dad and I still collected Petie and took him on the bus and, after school I still got a lift back with Ren's grandma and stayed at her house because Dad had a meeting.

"Ren's still not well, I'm afraid. She's tucked up in bed," Ren's grandma said.

I liked playing with Petie. For a while we played a card game. I think he was missing Snaffle. "It's a shame we can't play tennis," I said. "We've got racquets and tennis balls at home and we use the washing line as a net."

Ren's grandma said, "I think there are some badminton racquets upstairs. Petie would love having a game with you, Caspar, wouldn't you, Petie?"

Petie's eyes lit up. "Could we? If we play gently?"

Gran smiled. "I'm just concerned about my roses. But we could go over to the recreation ground. What do you think?"

"Yes," I said. "That sounds excellent. Shall I

fetch the racquets?"

Gran nodded. "Now, let me think. I moved them in the last clear-out. I'm sure they'll be in the trunk on the landing. It was Ren's dad's when he went to university. You'll just have to lift off the plant and put it on the floor. I know you're a very sensible boy."

"Leave it with me!" I called as I ran upstairs. The trunk on the landing was an old brown wooden one with a fancy embroidered cloth on top. It made me think of ships. I lifted off the plant and the decorated cloth and put them carefully on the floor beside it. When I pulled the lid open, it gave a big *creak*. Inside it were the kind of things people store for years and years: fabrics and ornaments and pairs of shoes with rubber bands round them. I sneezed. I couldn't see any racquets.

I like digging around in old boxes. You never know what you might find. It's like being an archaeologist, discovering the past. I found first one and then a second badminton racquet and one very chewed-up-looking shuttlecock. Maybe there were some more deeper down. I lifted out a heavy old book and opened the leather cover. The spine was sawdusty where the leather had worn off.

In the corner of the trunk a metal tin caught my eye. It was charcoal-coloured with imprints of pictures. I ran my hand across the top, my fingertips sinking into little pits in the metal. The lid was loose. I eased it off. A pen sat on top of some red and blue cloth. I knew that pen with its swirls in many colours of blue. My mouth opened in a big gasp.

How on earth?

I took it out. Unmistakably, definitely Jake's.

How did *that* get here? My brain was doing little flips and leaps. In Ren's house. In a trunk…

Then, suddenly, I felt a movement beside me.

"Caspar!"

"Ren!" I gasped. She stood over me in pyjamas, hair straggly. Like a zombie.

I ducked as if someone had thrown a ball at my head. Because her face had a shocked expression, eyes big and wide … mouth opening as if she was getting ready to shout. She was staring at the open tin. Her face turned to … angry. As if I was a burglar. "*What are you doing?*" Her voice was violent – like, *Explain yourself, you burglar person*. It felt as if I'd done something … terrible.

My brain couldn't make sense of it. "Oh, um, so, I hope you're better and we're playing downstairs except I came up and now…" I held out the pen, rolling it between my fingers. There was the little lever where you filled up the ink. And, along one edge, the initials JG in fancy script engraved into the metal. Jake Di Gambo. "This is Jake's pen," I said. "His special one. Look." I pointed to the initials. "JG."

Ren's shoulders twitched.

"I don't understand," I said. "Did Jake lend this to you?"

Ren stared at the pen as if she was deciding something very difficult and her mouth twisted up into small mouths and side mouths. I waited. "I found it," she murmured.

I turned the pen over in my hands. I felt squirmy inside. I remembered that day when the pencil box got passed round our class and I'd seen this pen and then it had … disappeared, like magic. Only it hadn't been magic … had it?

"I know where you got it. It was in the box of pencils that was passed round. You must have found it right after me because I saw it in there and I told everyone." My voice had changed to a different voice now. "I was sure that day. I was completely sure I'd seen it." She needed to explain. But her face was blank, like clay. I carried on. "But then you didn't say anything when Miss Chatto asked. She asked all of us, the whole class, if we'd seen it. And Jake asked too. And everyone was searching for ... *this.*"

Only Ren's eyes moved ... to the left and right.

I was feeling crosser and crosser. "So what's the answer? Why didn't you say you'd taken Jake's pen?"

Ren just stood there all paralysed.

Now I'd started I couldn't stop. "What about these other things in here?" I said, digging around.

"You're not supposed to be here," she said in a snappy voice.

My fingers had closed round... I looked up at Ren... Incredible! It was Miss Chatto's hairclip. "This is Miss Chatto's! Her silver one. She looked everywhere for this. You even helped her try to find it!" I gasped out.

Ren closed her eyes. That wasn't going to help!

I lifted out an old children's book with a horse

on the front. Inside the cover I flicked through to the school crest and stamp on a sheet for borrowing. "This is a school library book. Did you sign this out? Why is it in here?"

I looked up at her. "Ren, why have you got these things?"

She stayed still and stiff. "I don't remember," she said at last.

"What do you mean, you don't remember?" My voice was a shout now. "That sounds like rubbish! Did you take these things?"

"Stop it!"

She grabbed Jake's pen, the book and the clip, pushed them back inside the box and rammed the lid back on. She pulled the box close to her chest. "You shouldn't be here," she panted. "This is … nothing to do with you."

"You're changing the subject."

"You're a visitor. You shouldn't be here."

"And you're a thief!"

There was a terrible shocked silence.

Ren stared at me with a face of fury. "Leave these things alone. And leave me alone!" She pushed the dark metal box back into the corner of the trunk and rammed down the lid, and I only just pulled my hands away in time. "Why are you even here," she snapped, "snooping about?"

Sad furious feelings spun inside me. She was accusing *me*! "Your gran sent me. She said there were some badminton racquets in the trunk."

Ren sort of deflated. "Oh."

"That's why I'm here." I grabbed the racquets and leapt up. "I'm going back downstairs now. I wouldn't stay with you anyway."

"So go then."

"I'm going." I ran for the stairs.

"Good."

Chapter 32
Caspar

Out in the garden, playing with Petie at the recreation ground, all the rest of that day questions, questions in my head.

How could Ren steal other people's things? How could she? People she knew. People who were kind. I felt so angry. People had looked at me weirdly after Jake's pen disappeared. Miss Chatto had darted little looks at me, as if she didn't trust me. And all the time it had been Ren.

Miss Chatto was always kind to Ren.

Ren must be a really bad person. A monster. She must be. Only a bad person would do something like this. But Ren didn't seem bad. How could you be good some of the time and horrible the rest? I walked around in a haze of puzzles and questions. These stolen things were in a trunk in some weird metal tin. Why would she keep them like that? She was hurting people.

I carried the secret. It was very, very heavy. Ren was off school for another day and on her first day back she sat beside Petie on the bus in the morning and then her gran picked us up but dropped me back at home. I never saw Ren on her own all day in school. I think she was avoiding me.

My thoughts went round and round. Should I tell a grown-up?

I thought about bank robbers and the requests for information the police put on lamp posts. I had information. I knew a thing… It had turned into *my* secret, not just Ren's. And I didn't want it.

I'd never had any kind of secret before. When I was little, if I broke something – like when I made an obstacle course for Snaffle from random things, and he got tangled up in Dad's new headphones and dragged them round the banisters and snapped them – I just said to Mum and Dad, "I'm really sorry." Because I was. I didn't keep the bad thing secret for even, like, ten minutes! It was Snaffle's fault but mine too. And I saved up for new headphones and I bought them. Because he's my dad. Miss Chatto hadn't done anything wrong. She didn't deserve to lose her silver hairclip, did she?

And Jake's pen. Jake was a really good artist. And that was the pen he used. It helped him be an artist. Ren wasn't even using it.

This was so bad and wrong. I couldn't sit still in my bedroom. I paced around. I couldn't let this carry on. I had to do something. I had to make things better.

Maybe I should talk to Mum and Dad? But then Ren would get into massive trouble and it would be my fault. I thought about the fire and her house burning down. Ren must still be so sad about her house. I would be making everything worse. And she was my friend, wasn't she?

No she wasn't.

Well, she had been.

Well, she wasn't now.

No, but ... what should a friend do?

Chapter 33
Ren

Caspar was a snooper. He was.

I sat back in bed. My heart was beating hard.

I thought about his face when he had looked up at me. Frowny and sad. Holding Jake's pen.

He was upset. I'd made him upset.

I flung myself around on the bed. My head felt hot.

Stop thinking about Caspar.

He was a snooper, so it was his fault that he found out.

Collecting was the only thing I was good at. I had light fingers, like air.

He shouldn't have opened the Shadowbox. It was completely his fault he did that. Something had been ruined. Another thought hit me; he thought I was a bad person now. No, he *knew* I was a bad person. Bad inside. Like a poisoned apple. He shouldn't be with a bad person like me. Probably he wouldn't talk to me any more. I was too bad to be with.

I couldn't rest. My heart thumped. I kept remembering his sad face when he saw inside the box.

And another thing: what would he do now that he knew? Would he say he didn't want to come to Gran's any more? Would he find an excuse and stop coming round for tea?

I gulped. And then, of course, now *he knew* … what if he told on me, told them *everything*?

I got up and went down the corridor. The door to Gran's room was a little bit open. Yes! She'd forgotten to lock it. Or she was in there? I peeped inside. No, the room was empty. My heart pounded. At last! I headed in.

There was a smell in the air like roses. I stared at the flowery bedspread, the bookcases lining the walls, the pottery things on shelves and the huge wardrobe. There, in the far corner, was the cupboard of shining things I had glimpsed before.

I felt the beat inside me, the finger twitch. In seconds I was rushing across to the cupboard, kneeling down. So many small things sat in rows inside: shining glass, bright silver, small framed pictures, carvings.

I turned the little key and eased open the door.

The sound of voices carried from downstairs. *Be quick!* My fingers closed round something. I softly closed and locked the door and sped back across the rug, disappearing like smoke back on to the landing.

No one came upstairs.

It was a bird, as small as a robin but skinny, with twig-like legs and real yellow and blue feathers. So light. A bird made from real feathers. I ran the tip of my finger over its bright beady eye. It was like Gran: scratchy and sharp. Watching me. You couldn't hug it.

I felt calmer now. I added the bird to the Shadowbox. Gran deserved to lose it; she was always cross at me.

The warm buzz came. That was clever. Then I went back to bed.

But the calm didn't last. I tossed and turned. I thought of Caspar again. What a stupid thing to nose around. If he had left my box alone instead of nosing about, snooping about…

He would never speak to me again. I'd lost him.

And when he told them, they'd say I shouldn't be in a normal school with normal children and send me away to a special type of school for a bad person…

I lay and sweated.

That night my dream came again. My fingers were gripping the edge of my bedroom floor as the flames licked my legs. Don't fall. Don't fall into the flames and the dark.

And a voice was calling. My eyes snapped open in the brown spare room. "Ren … Ren." Petie was awake and moaning.

"Ren, tell me about Mr Softie," he called from his bed on the other side of the room.

Not Mr Softie. Not again!

Anger surged inside me. "No. Go to sleep."

"Please, Ren, tell me where he is today."

"Leave me alone." I felt like a bear in a cave that had been poked with a stick.

Petie kept prattling on. "Mr Softie went to Africa

and he saw lions with Flynn. He rode on a zebra and held on with his paws. And then he drove the racing car… You said. Ren, tell me. What is he doing now?"

"I don't know." The hot angry bear rose up. "I think … she lost him." My voice was cold. Why was everything so bad and difficult and wrong? Why was I bad? "Someone took him," I heard myself say. "A big dark shape. They put him in a bag."

Petie gasped. "No, Ren! You said he was all right."

"He's not now. He's gone."

"He can't be," Petie bleated out in the dark.

"I'm sick of your stupid Mr Softie," I said. "I'm going to sleep."

"But he was there," Petie sobbed.

"Well, he isn't now."

Silence.

"Maybe he was never there," I heard myself say. "Maybe he was in the fire after all."

"Don't say that."

"Maybe he got burned. Maybe his yellow fur went brown and fell out … then he was gone. *Fuff!* In the fire."

Petie was crying. "Noo."

I pulled the pillow over my head. "Leave me alone. Go to sleep." I held the pillow there. I stayed like that a long time. I think I actually did fall asleep.

Sometime later my pillow rolled away on to the floor and I woke up.

Petie must be asleep by now. I flicked the night light on to check. I jumped out of bed and crossed the room.

His bed was empty.

Chapter 34
Ren

Seconds later I was out of the door and down the stairs. I checked the living room and kitchen and he wasn't in there. My heart raced. I unhooked a fleece from beside the door, pulled it on and ran out into the night. An icy blast hit me. I should have put shoes on. Too late now. The gritty ground hurt my feet and turned them to blocks of ice.

I must find him.

My breath came in big gulps. Which way?

Beside the house, the caravan was in darkness.

Should I wake Mum and Dad?

No way. Think how angry they'd be. *We trusted*

you, Ren! I rushed silently by.

Ow, ow. I hobbled over the scratchy stones, out of the driveway and down the road. The whole street was dark and still with a few street lights casting pools of gold. It was completely, scarily empty. I was panicking now. This was mad. This was impossible and mad. Where was he?

My painful feet turned numb. Chill air forced its way into my pyjamas. Argh! I tried to stop my teeth chattering.

I rushed on. How far could he have got while I was sleeping?

So I ran. Could I be wrong? Could Petie still be in Gran's house? But I had a terrible feeling he would make for our burned-down house. He'd never get there, though; it was miles away. He would just get lost. And then what?

My teeth ground and chattered. It was so cold!

I ran right up the road and turned the corner. And then I spotted the little barefoot figure in pale pyjamas, lit up, just turning the corner by the postbox.

I gasped, racing to get to him. "Petie!"

He turned and saw me, but he didn't stop.

I caught up with him just past the corner and

grabbed him. His face was pinched. “You go away,” he sobbed.

“Petie, I’m really sorry. I don’t know why I said that thing. I’m so sorry.”

“I’m going home to find Mr Softie,” he said, wrenching his arms away.

I grabbed him again. “It’s all right. I’ve got you now. And it’s OK – you don’t need to go.”

He stood doubtfully, staring up at me from his tear-streaked face. “I have to. Mr Softie’s only got me.”

I was crying too. “No, he hasn’t. He’s got both of us.” I hugged Petie then. His cheek was ice-cold.

“You don’t care about him. You said he was gone.”

I looked into his desperate little worried face. It was my fault.

“I’m sorry. I really am!” Words flew from my mouth. “I’ll show you... Mr Softie will be home tomorrow!”

Petie’s mouth opened wide then shut. He shook his head. “I don’t believe you, Ren.”

“He will!” I pulled the fleece over both of us and turned him round. I could feel his little body shuddering against me. We set off. He let himself be walked back. "Mr Softie's coming. You'll see. It's going to be OK."

I couldn't talk any more; I was too cold and sad and sobbing. I had to get him back and warm and safe. I thought of what might have happened if I hadn't found him and I felt more horrified then than when I had realised he was gone. When we reached Gran's front door we half fell inside.

"Shush," I said. If Gran woke, I'd be in terrible trouble. Mum and Dad would be bound to blame me.

We sneaked upstairs. Petie sat in my bed and I rubbed his legs and arms. They felt like little icy rods. His feet were gritty. I rubbed them on a towel. I didn't care about anything except warming him up. I felt so bad, so, so bad. I was the worst person. We got into my bed and he pushed his cold feet against me. I didn't push them away.

He started to warm up. "What time?" he asked.

I looked over at my phone. "It's one o'clock in the morning," I whispered.

"Not now. I mean, what time will Mr Softie be home?"

"Later."

"But today?"

"Yes, today."

Petie curled on his side and I curled round him. I breathed in his hair. He felt small and real. He was back. He was safe. My little brother. He was only five. He made me so cross and mad. We fought so much. And yet, right then, I realised that I didn't hate having Petie with me as much as I'd hated losing him.

Chapter 35
Ren

The next day I put the towel and dirty sheets in the washing machine. Gran said, "I'm glad to see you being more grown-up." She must have thought Petie had wet the bed again.

I nodded. "Oh, and do you need any shopping, Gran?"

"This is encouraging, Ren," she said. She dug in her purse for money. "You could get some more milk. Two pints. Take your phone and keep it switched on."

I wandered past the arcade and saw the toyshop with the smartly dressed dolls in its window. That's where we had bought him. Mr Softie had been my present to Petie when he was born. He was machine-washable – a little bear with pale-brown fur that was very soft and a stitched smile. Safe, Dad had said. Safe enough to give to your new brother straight away. The other cuddly bears were too large and Petie wouldn't have been able to hold them. "Some of these are bigger than him!" Dad had said, as we had looked along the rows of teddies in outfits and hats.

When we got to the hospital, Dad turned out to be right. My new baby brother was really small and red-faced. Mum said to tuck the teddy in his cot beside him. The baby was in a see-through cot, like a goldfish in a bowl. I hardly dared go near him; he looked so little and helpless.

"What shall we call him?" Dad asked, and I thought he was talking to me, so I said, "Mr Softie," and everyone laughed, even the nurse.

"I meant the baby!" Dad said.

Mum laughed too. "Imagine having a baby brother called Mr Softie! What a funny idea!"

But the name stuck. Petie had carried Mr Softie around ever since. He had been on every holiday and trip away from home. He had listened to every story and been dropped in the weirdest places.

There was no point going inside the smart toyshop. That lady looking out of the window at me would probably follow me around, asking if she could help. I didn't want people. I wanted my tingling fingers. I wanted what I was good at.

I noticed the shop next door to the toyshop. It had lights on but it was much gloomier. I realised I had been in there before too. It was a charity shop. Cancer Research.

I pushed the door and it dinged as I went inside. I found myself in a gloomy room packed with racks of clothes, shoes by the wall and crockery and candles. It smelled stale. It was a mixture of sweat and perfume. The children's bit was at the back.

There were two other people in the shop. One of them, a lady with a wheelie shopping trolley, was talking to the lady at the till. I skirted round her and headed for the back.

Someone called, "Hello, sweetheart."

"I told her not to, but she never listens," said the shopping lady.

"You'd think she'd learn," said the lady on the till. She had a bright-pink jumper and big round glasses that caught the light.

"Her sort never do," said the trolley lady.

I'd reached the back now. Some children's toys were on the shelf: a set of bricks and some books for babies. Then, near the racks of clothes, I spotted a deep basket that said *All items £2.*

My fingers tingled. I started to look through it: hats, balled-up socks and scarves. I checked the women again, but they were still chatting. I was hidden by the ladies' dresses. I dug deeper: a rattle, more socks and gloves, a bib with rabbits on. Then, near the bottom, a small teddy. It was just the right size for Mr Softie. Similar fur and fabric body. But this bear was dark red.

I hesitated. I was lucky to find him. *Quick. Don't worry about the colour.*

The buzz inside me began to build. My breaths came fast.

There was a noise near me. I shoved the little bear up my sleeve.

"Are you OK there, love?" The woman from the till in the pink jumper with the big round glasses had come right up beside me.

"I'm looking for…" I pretended to search the basket. "I can't find… I'm looking for something for my brother."

My heart pounded like crazy. I forced a smile. "I don't think there's anything here he would like."

"Are you sure?" She stared at me hard. "How old is he?"

I stepped back. "Oh, um, five."

She hadn't seen. She couldn't have. "He sounds a bit old for the bricks then," she said, pointing to the toys on the shelf.

The bear might drop out. I could feel the lump of it inside my cuff. "I have to go. My mum's waiting."

I set off back across the shop, behind the racks of clothes.

The trolley lady was staring at me too. The bear up my sleeve felt hot, itchy. *Don't touch it. Don't push it further up. Just get out!*

"Thanks anyway!" I grabbed the door.

Get out, get out.

On to the street. Panting. *Get out of sight. Don't check. Walk don't run.*

I did it! The lump in my sleeve poked into my arm.

I didn't look at it all the way home.

I was so good at this.

I pictured that pink-jumper lady following me out of the shop and chasing me back across the shopping centre. I imagined hands clutching me…

I pictured her all the rest of the way home. But it was OK. Nothing happened and the streets were busy with families and buses as usual.

I walked quickly. I looked behind me. No one.

Slower. My heart cooled.

Those things in the basket weren't special. The red bear had been with the old pairs of socks – things no one wanted. I sped up, bought the milk for Gran and headed home.

Petie would be happy. I would think of a way to explain about the colour.

I tore off the price tag and gave the replacement Mr Softie to Petie. "He's back," I said.

"He looks different," Petie said, stroking the dark-red fur.

"His fur got changed in the fire," I said. "He went too near the flames."

Petie tested the fur with one finger. Then he gripped the bear in both hands. "You're home now," he whispered, holding him to his cheek.

At teatime he told Dad. "Ren got Mr Softie back." He held out the little bear and let Dad stroke him before snatching him back. "No! You can't have him. He's mine!"

Dad was staring at me intently. "Is this true, love?"

"I … I… Petie needed him back," I said.

Dad steered me away so Petie couldn't hear us. "Where did you buy it?"

"I got it … in town," I murmured.

Dad nodded firmly. "That's one of the nicest things you've ever done for your brother. I am so proud of you, Ren!"

I squirmed. "No, Dad, don't be … it's not … I'm not…"

But Dad pushed his hand in his pocket and handed me all his change. "You shouldn't have to pay for a present for your brother. What a lovely sister, though."

"No. Don't give me anything!"

"Nonsense. You've been so kind. She's a great sister, isn't she, Petie?"

Dad told Mum and Gran about it too.

They all said what a great sister I was.

My insides flipped around like snakes in a bag. I was a person who was all wrong. Dad had paid me back when I hadn't spent any money in the first place.

I put Dad's handful of money in the Shadowbox

and shut the lid.

"Can we still have the stories, though?" Petie said, as we went to bed that evening.

"But Mr Softie's back!"

"But he's been away. He's had lots of adventures."

"Maybe *you* can tell the stories?" I said.

Petie frowned. "You're better at the stories, Ren," he said. "You know where he's been."

Chapter 36
Caspar

I hadn't decided what to do about Ren and my discovery and it plagued me.

Also, I had another worry, another thing I thought I had seen. I had had a glimpse of something bright red in that box. I thought I knew what it was, but I needed to check.

At playtime I sat down next to Shabbir. "Hiya."

He turned his head slowly. "Oh, hi, Caspar."

He's not allowed to run around, so he's always sitting near the water fountain.

"Are you still painting your stones?" I asked.

"Yeah." He sounded a bit flat, even for Shabbir.

"That ladybird one, the one you showed us, can I have another look at it?" I asked.

Shabbir breathed in. He screwed up his nose and blinked a few times. Shabbir looked a lot like my grandad, when his eyes didn't seem to focus.

"I can't find the ladybird stone, Caspar," he said.

My insides squirmed. "Oh!"

"It must be somewhere," Shabbir said.

"Did you tell anyone that you couldn't find it?" I asked.

"No." He pushed his glasses up his nose. "I'm always losing things, Caspar."

"Maybe your stone's somewhere in school?" This was hurting me. I had a strong feeling about where that stone was. A really strong feeling. "I expect it will turn up," I said.

He smiled. "Yeah. I expect it will."

"I know it was your best one."

"Yeah, it was."

I'd been right. I felt grim and sure. That afternoon after school I stayed at Ren's grandma's before Dad collected me, the way I often did, but this time I said to Ren, "Come upstairs. I have something to say to you that won't wait."

I marched her upstairs, opened the trunk, dumping the plant and cloth on the floor beside it.

"What are you doing?" she asked crossly.

I ignored her and dug around inside the box. Sure enough, I felt a round, cool, smooth object.

I brought out Shabbir's painted ladybird. "Look," I said. "This must have taken Shabbir hours to paint."

Ren looked, but only a tiny peep then she turned away.

I grabbed her arm. "No. Look properly."

I held her tight. "Look at what you took. I've been thinking and thinking. I don't think I've ever thought so much about anything *ever.*"

A tear dripped off her nose.

"You took Shabbir's ladybird. His own thing that he made!"

"I thought..." Her voice was gravelly.

I was so cross now. "You thought WHAT?"

She gulped. "I thought if I took it, it might ... give me some of his luck. He said it was lucky. He might have lots of stones. He ... might not even notice."

Anger boiled in me. "Well, you're wrong. I

asked Shabbir and he told me he's been looking for it. He was proud of it. Now he's worrying about it. You've made him sad."

Ren's head drooped. Her shoulders shook. "I get sad," she murmured.

"So? I got sad when Matty went away to university. But I didn't *steal* things."

"That's different. At least your brother comes home." Her voice was small and squashed. "I'm not anyone any more."

We stayed there all miserable.

"You're still you. Of course you're you, Ren," I said. "These things you took belong to other people. You can't just have them."

She was all flopped down. Like a toy with no stuffing.

"Snaffle takes food," I said. "But the difference is that makes him happy. You aren't. With Snaffle it's funny. It's only food. Plus, he's a dog. With Snaffle we all laugh and he eats the things and they're gone. But the box you've got – well, what are you going to do with it?"

I put Shabbir's ladybird back in Ren's weird tin box. We sat for a while. I felt mean, but still I carried on. "You can't take someone else's luck,

Ren. Shabbir painted those stones himself … for him. He's been, like, not well at all, and he's still quite … worn out."

"Stop talking about him," she whispered.

"No, Ren. I have to. You can't keep it. It would be wrong. Think how hard Shabbir worked on it. It's making me feel sick … and sad. It's terrible."

She turned to look at me. Tears streaked her face. "*You* feel terrible?"

"Yes, I've been worrying and worrying. I don't know what to do, Ren."

"You haven't told anyone, have you?" she asked in a small voice.

"No. Not yet. But… I can't stop thinking about it. And Shabbir feels bad. And Jake must too about his pen. Miss Chatto must. You're hurting these people and you have to stop."

She gulped.

"And … and … you don't even want the things. It's mad."

"But I don't know how to stop!" she sobbed.

"Just stop. Think about the people they belong to."

"And what about the Shadowbox things I already took?"

"Shadowbox?"

We both looked at the tin with all the stolen things spilling out of it.

Ren nodded. "It used to be our biscuit tin ... at home." She sniffed. "It's all burned. They gave it back to us after the fire. Petie called it a shadowbox."

A voice called from downstairs. "Ren!" It was Petie.

We pushed the things back in without looking at each other.

Chapter 37
Caspar

That evening I asked Mum, just in a chatty kind of way, "What should you do if you have something that's not yours ... taken from someone?"

"What's this about, Caspar?"

When it came out, my voice was shaking as if I was the thief. "Someone took a book from our school library and they didn't sign the borrowing book or scan it and put the card in."

"Oh, I see, well, they should put it back, I suppose. I mean, it should go back," she said.

I nodded. I felt much better. "Yes, that's right," I said. "That's easy to sort out."

So I had the answer; I couldn't let the box stay at Ren's gran's house any longer.

Next day after school, when Ren was chatting to her dad in the caravan and the coast was clear, I took a folded-up bag from my pocket and tipped the contents of the Shadowbox into it. The bag was a soft fabric one from our butcher at Christmas, free with the turkey. It said *Season's Greetings* on the side and had a line of poppers along the top to fasten it. I left a note inside the Shadowbox for Ren to find. I didn't know what I was going to do with the things, but getting them out of the house was step one. I think sometimes you have to take step one because you know it's the right step, even if you don't know all the other steps yet. Your heart tells you. As I packed the Shadowbox in the butcher's bag I felt as if there was no going back. I imagined myself walking into town and putting the bag in a bin so Ren wouldn't have the things to make her sad any more. But those things belonged to people. I wondered what it was like to get arrested. I felt guilty even just carrying the bag, like the things were screaming at me. Like in *Jack and the Beanstalk* when the stolen harp is shouting out,

"Hey, hey!" and Jack is running faster and faster, and the giant is coming after him in huge strides. "Fee-fi-fo-fum, give back what you took from me!"

Dad collected me and we set off home. "How was your day?" he asked as we crossed at the lights.

I cradled the large bag in my hands. Its poppers kept bursting open. "Stressful," I said.

"What's in your bag?"

"I'd rather not talk about it."

"You're panting. Are you OK, Caspar?"

We crossed the zebra crossing. "You know how you said you sometimes have to do step one because you know it's right even if you're not sure what steps two and three are?" I said.

Dad grinned. "Did I say that?"

"Don't smile."

"And you don't want to talk about it?"

"No."

"You've got a look on your face that says you mean business, Caspar. You don't have to bite your lip quite so hard."

"I do have to."

"OK, OK, let's talk about supper. Do you think you can manage to talk about that?"

"Yep."

"Spaghetti?"

"OK."

"Dog walk before bed?"

"Good plan!"

Here's what I was thinking: most of the things had been taken in school so they needed to go back to school. I wanted Ren to put them back. *She* must put them back and not me, because she took them. Some of them I didn't know who the owner had been anyway. I could help her. She should put them back ASAP, urgently. I would be her cheering-in-the-background supporter, a bit like when Matty ran the half-marathon and we all waited by the finish line with Snaffle.

I wrote myself a list of ways to transport the things to school:

1. Wear a big coat of Matty's and put the stolen things in the pockets. But then if I tried to keep that on in school, it would be too obvious.
2. Pack a rucksack and wrap the things so they looked like birthday presents. Too complicated.
3. Say it was my *My Life in a Box* project if anyone asked. Best answer.

I knew what I had to do.

Chapter 38
Ren

I found a note from Caspar in the Shadowbox that evening. It was the only thing in the box. Everything had gone. I stood holding the scrap of paper, my hand shaking.

I HAVE GOT THE THINGS FROM THE BOX.

YOU SAID YOU HATE THE STEALING AND I HATE IT TOO.

I DON'T WANT YOU TO STEAL ANY MORE. I THINK IT IS LIKE POISON (REALLY BAD!!!).

PLEASE STOP. I WILL HELP YOU. SEE YOU TOMORROW AT SCHOOL.

YOUR FRIEND, CASPAR

Chapter 39
Caspar

I had a sort of plan.

I would locate the shoebox I had decorated for the *My Life in a Box* project in our classroom and put the bag of stolen things in it. This would be a *temporary measure*. We weren't supposed to be finishing our boxes this week, but I could just look keen and the butcher's bag of things could stay in it, firmly fastened along the top. Then I had to persuade Ren to sneak all the things back to their owners, *undercover*. It should work.

I hugged the butcher's bag inside my coat, a great big lump with lots of sticking-out bits. I walked extra slowly and kept my elbows out. I had persuaded Dad to take Ren and Petie without me and let me get the earlier bus on my own because I had things to do when I got to school. When I arrived, Mrs Ellis popped her head out of the office. "Morning, Caspar. Gracious, what have you got there?"

I tried to close my coat but I didn't have any spare hands. "It's for … it's involving … you know, the project in our class…" I said, bowing my head low.

Things mustn't stick out. She mustn't see. I was sweating.

"Do you want to leave some things in the office?"

"I … no, definitely not." I rushed away up the corridor.

Then the tricky bit! I took off my coat in the cloakroom and hung it up.

Inside the corridor I hoisted the crammed butcher's bag into my arms. *Visible. So visible!* People were barging into me, rushing to be in time to play football before the bell for registration. I made it to our classroom and went to Miss Chatto's art cupboard at the back where we had left our boxes drying yesterday.

Disaster! The shelves were empty. Our decorated boxes weren't there!

I swung round. "Where are our *box full of me* boxes?" I asked Mr Charles, our classroom assistant, who was standing at the front.

"They've been moved to the art room. They need to be bone dry before anything goes in them. Some people went a bit wild with the glue," he said. "And you should be outside, Caspar."

Oh no. Oh no. My plan was in bits! "But I need to get to my box now," I said. My mind was whirring. Panic filled me. "I know my box is dry. Can I go and ... visit it?"

"Not now. Since you're early, just sit down and get out your reading book."

I still stood there. Where else could I put the butcher's bag? It had to be safe! Standing there with it in my arms was ... *high risk.*

"Caspar!"

"Sorry. I've got things on my mind," I said.

"I beg your pardon! Sit down, Caspar," Mr Charles said.

"Sorry."

"And put your things in your desk."

My things. *Oh no, they aren't mine*, I nearly said. In the desk?? No! Desks weren't safe. But where else was there? Maybe I should hang the butcher's bag under my coat in the cloakroom. Would that be safer?

"Back in a minute," I said. "I think I'll just—"

"Caspar! How many times? Just get out your reading book."

The bell went outside.

My class began to come in. They jostled and chatted. "Seats, everyone," Mr Charles called.

My face glowed. I stuffed the bag in my desk but there was so much in it that I couldn't shut the desk lid properly. I lay over it. I stuck my hands out straight and tried to turn the pages of my book.

Ren came in and sat down on the other side of the classroom. She glanced over at me then bent over her desk. I didn't want to leave my desk *unguarded* but I had to talk to her. I was feeling very stressed. By now Miss Chatto had come in and she and Mr Charles were talking by the whiteboard.

I sank down on the floor and began crawling over to where Ren was.

She stared over at me with panic in her eyes.

"What are you doing?" she mouthed.

"Caspar, what on earth are you doing?" called Miss Chatto from the front.

"Crawling," I said.

Everyone laughed.

Miss Chatto sighed sharply and muttered something.

Mr Charles said, "Right, Caspar, that's enough. You come with me. Now!"

"But I can't," I said.

I couldn't leave the bag!

"Now, Caspar!" Mr Charles marched me out of the classroom.

Anyone could find out Ren's secret and discover the stolen things now. My class were always messing about with the desks, flinging open the lids and pulling things out. And the lid wasn't even shut properly.

Mr Charles took me to the tables in the corridor where people did extra reading. I had to get back to my desk. I had to. I was frantic with worry.

I wondered if my heart might be having to beat too hard because it really seemed to be pounding like a storm inside me. The major reason was that I had realised a thing that I suppose I had known all along really, but now in school with Mr Charles getting the reading book out and beginning to read it quietly to me, which would never work because my heart was louder than the story words and just pounding and pounding and sweat was breaking out on my hands, I had realised this: I couldn't lie. I couldn't say things that weren't true, even to protect Ren. Something inside me wouldn't let me. So I couldn't get her out of trouble and I might be about to get her into a lot more.

I imagined Miss Chatto throwing open my desk, calling, "What's in this bag, Caspar?" and me shouting back, "Stolen stuff. I'm carrying it for a friend."

All the faces in my class would be frozen in expressions of shock and horror. *Stolen!*

Chapter 40
Caspar

I couldn't talk to Ren for the first part of the morning. I kept making a desperate face over at her, but she always had her head turned away. My brain was in agony! I got every question wrong in maths. Underneath me, the bag in my desk made the desktop tilt at a wonky angle. I had to keep spreading myself across it to keep the things safe inside.

When break finally came, everyone rushed outside and I realised Ren had gone out too. I must talk to her! But, big problem, I couldn't just abandon the bag! I went to the window and tried to see Ren in the crowds. Why hadn't she stayed inside with me? I was all alone with the bag and the problem.

And then major doubts started ambushing me. Ren had said she wanted the stolen things to be gone. She'd said the things made her sad, same as me. But she hadn't agreed to put everything back, had she? So... My insides quaked. My heart was doing flips. What if Ren refused to do anything *at all*?

I was going to have to move the bag. Instinct told me that under my coat in the cloakroom would be safer. Nobody spent any time in the cloakroom, especially now we weren't supposed to be inside at breaks and lunchtimes.

Oh, Caspar, I suddenly thought, *you should be outside right now. You're drawing attention to yourself.*

I rushed back to my desk and grabbed the butcher's bag from inside it. It was extremely difficult to support the bag underneath with one hand while trying to grapple the poppers shut with the other. It was a stupid bag. It kept bursting open. Why had I chosen this useless bag?

I headed for the door. I would find my coat. I

would hide the bag. I would get hold of Ren at lunchtime. It would be OK.

I swung the classroom door open, looking down at the bag. *Woomph!* Someone had pushed the door forcefully from the other side.

I flew backwards. The bag burst open and something fell out and hit the floor. I yelped.

The person who had come in was Jake.

The thing that had hit the floor was a water bottle.

Disaster!!!

I staggered to my feet, clutching the butcher's bag. The flask was still rolling and came to a stop right by Jake's green suede boot. Jake's eyes went wide. His mouth pinched. He picked up the thing and turned it over. "Is this yours?" The bottle was a copper colour with a shiny sprinkle surface. "Hang on, Caspar – isn't this the bottle we were all looking for a few days ago, the one you and I talked about?"

A rabbit in headlights on a motorway. That was me. "Yes," I whispered.

Jake frowned. "It's Ellie's?"

I nodded.

Jake's eyes rested on the bag in my arms.

"So...?"

I put my hand over the top of the bag to stop more things falling out.

"I think you and I need to have a chat." Jake's voice was hard and brisk.

I looked around desperately, but Jake had already set off across the classroom to Miss Chatto's art cupboard at the back. His coat flowed behind him.

I followed him in. The art cupboard was full of materials: paints and big bottles of glue.

"Things have been going walkabout in your class ... and now this! What else is in that bag, Caspar?"

I gulped. "Urgh..."

He looked at the bag in my arms and then his eyes moved up and fixed on mine. "Are those things you are carrying yours? Are they for our project?"

I pictured myself throwing glue at Jake from one of the big bottles. But why would I do that? Anyway, the lids were quite hard to get off.

"No," I said. "They're not mine."

"So...?"

"Um."

"What else is in that bag, buddy?"

I was feeling very boxed in. Jake was staring at me and there was literally nowhere to hide.

"Um, well."

"Give me the bag. I need to look in it."

"Actually, please could you not?" I said.

"We're going to have to talk about this. Or I'm going to have to report it."

"I can't tell you anything." I felt as if I was staring into a deep dark hole and slowly falling inside it. I couldn't tell him about Ren. I couldn't make things worse for Ren.

Chapter 41
Caspar

Shouts carried from the playground. Jake and I stood there in the cupboard. I wished I was anywhere else but here. I clutched the bag to me. I wanted to *defend* it.

"I like you, Caspar. You seem like a good kid," Jake said.

"Thank you."

"Caspar...?"

"I actually can't explain."

Jake kept staring. His eyes seemed to drill inside my brain.

The cupboard door came open. It was Ren. I

shook my head and rolled my eyes at her.

She'll blame me, I suddenly thought. *Of course she will. She'll say she knows nothing about the bag of stolen things. Then what? I'll be expelled. Everyone will know. We'll have to move house!*

Ren shook. Her shoulders rose up, her body pitching forward like a runner, her mouth trembling.

Here we go. I was definitely doomed.

She stared at the bag in my arms and over to the water bottle in Jake's hands then back to the bag. "Don't be angry with Caspar. It's not his fault," she said, loud and firm. Then her face sort of crumbled.

Jake reeled back. "Two of you! What the hell is going on?" he muttered. "I'm going to have to report this." There was a shunting noise as some paints fell off the shelf behind him. The cupboard was a bit small for three people.

"No!" Ren said very loudly. She closed her eyes. Her head was bowed.

Jake ran his hands through his hair. "This is totally out of order. You're on a knife edge here, a total knife edge. I should go and get your teacher right now."

"I agree," I said, "but the thing is … it's a mistake. It's a great big fat mistake."

Jake's eyes flicked to me. "Don't say anything, Caspar." He was staring at Ren.

"I know it looks bad," I said, "but—"

Jake's hand sliced the air. "JUST STOP TALKING, Caspar!"

Everything went still. The noise of the playground surged outside the cupboard. "Gooooaalll!" someone shouted.

Jake went on looking expectantly at Ren.

Her head slowly came up. She was crying now, shaking. A groan came from her like the saddest person. Her fingers reached out for the shelf beside her, and she held on to it like she might melt and fall away. Her mouth twisted and she took a huge breath. "It was me. I took those things," she said.

Jake muttered something. His hand swept the air, and I knew he still didn't want me to speak.

I listened to the shouts and calls outside and the *thunk* each time the football hit the wall.

Tears poured down Ren's cheeks. She gulped. "It was wrong," she said. "I know it was wrong. I just felt so sad. I didn't have any things … like of my own. Because of the fire. All my things. Everything was just … gone." She heaved big sobs. "I didn't even want those things. I just … kept taking them. I don't really know why. I don't."

She went on crying. It really hurt to watch her, just to watch her and not do anything. I decided it was safe to speak. "We'll put everything back," I told Jake. "Every single thing."

Ren nodded. "Yes. That's right. I know that … we have to put the things back."

"We'll put them back fast," I said. "Like literally today … mostly."

There was silence in the cupboard. "This is unbelievable. I could lose my job," Jake said. He tugged at his beard.

"Please," Ren said. She sniffed. "I promise."

Jake stared at her. "Mmm."

My heart pounded. What would he do?

"Just give us until after the weekend. That's only a few days," I said.

"I'd be putting my neck on the line. This is a huge thing you're asking."

"No one will know," I said. "We'll keep schtum!"

Jake stared at me. A big gasp came out. He seemed to pull himself up taller. It was like a trial where the judge says, "GUILTY!"

He put his hand to his forehead and sighed a huge sigh. He looked at Ren, then at me, then at Ren again. His lips pulled together tight, like someone getting ready to drink poison. "Right … OK … OK … Monday."

Ren nodded.

"Yes," I said.

"Fix it," he said.

The bell went and we all jumped.

Jake shook himself. He pulled down the cuffs on his coat. "Monday. Come and tell me it's all done on Monday."

"Yes," we both said.

After Jake left, Ren and I stood in the cupboard.

It was the end of break. Any second our class would come thundering in from the playground.

"Right," I said. "So … we are in a place of extreme danger. We have to get on with it. We need a strategy, Ren."

She nodded.

"The things that are from this classroom, we can put back at lunchtime. We'll both do it." I thought for a second. "Actually, no. You have to do it because you took the things, but I'll help."

Ren bit her lips.

"It's the only way," I said, "and the other things we can do bit by bit in the next two days. No one must see us put things back. Definitely no one must thank us for their things. If people thank us and think we found the things, that would be wrong," I said. "We can only make it right by doing it in secret."

"Yes," she said.

"We'll be like reverse criminals."

We hid the bag in the art cupboard, behind the paints, nodded to each other and separated at the door. The rest of the morning we ignored each other and tried to be normal. It was still hard to concentrate.

I kept picturing the putting back, and the putting-back places were always empty. It was quiet, like a film set. But it might not turn out like that. We might get caught and the person who found us would assume we were pinching the things and not putting them back. Nobody in the whole history of the world was famous for putting things back – they were always famous for stealing them!

Chapter 42

Caspar

My mind went over what we would need to do at lunchtime. First, Ren should replace the things she had taken from our own classroom, but it would be hard to get inside at lunchtime because we weren't allowed due to the recent thefts. There always seemed to be adults prowling around.

As soon as we'd had eaten our packed lunches, sitting on a bench outside, we both went inside again. Ren went into our classroom and I was the door guard. "The bag's in the art cupboard. Be quick," I said.

"What if someone comes?"

"Leave that with me. If anyone comes, I'll keep them talking," I said.

Ren had just disappeared inside when the outside door banged and one of the playground supervisors, Mrs Anthony, came in. She saw me. "You should be outside, Caspar," she said.

"I know," I said. Now what? I couldn't abandon Ren. Mrs Anthony might march straight in and see Ren putting things back. I had to keep her talking. "Did you know that we're making boxes with an artist called Jake?" I asked her.

Her eyes narrowed. "Outside. Now," she said.

I opened my locker. "Just a sec…" I turned and her scowling face was very near. "Have you ever thought about making a box all about you, Mrs Anthony? What would you put in it?"

"I'd put you in it at the rate you're going. Now, out!"

"I will go," I said. "It's just…" Now what could I say? "Do you like your job?"

"Not always, no." She looked annoyed now. She folded her arms across her chest. If I had a boxing match with Mrs Anthony, I think she would win it.

I rested my arm across the top of the locker.

"Do you ever think maybe our lockers are a bit small for all the things we need, because I do."

"Do you?" Her face was getting redder.

"Yes. Personally I would like one much bigger."

"Some schools don't have lockers at all, you know. They're a privilege."

Mrs Anthony is quite a miserable person. When she's on playground duty, her face looks as if she's eaten something that's gone off.

"That's interesting, about other schools," I said. "I'll be gone in a minute; I'm just collecting something."

Her mouth set firm. "Five team points are about to be lost. Five … four … three … two—"

I still stood there. "Do you worry about climate change, Mrs Anthony?"

"Right. That's enough. You're about to be in big trouble."

Our classroom door opened and Ren appeared. She spotted Mrs Anthony.

I pulled my hat out of my locker. "I knew it was in there somewhere. Have a nice afternoon!"

I rushed away down the corridor, following Ren outside, leaving Mrs Anthony standing there.

Chapter 43
Ren

There was no special feeling in my hands in the putting back. I felt twisty and nervous right up to the last minute.

While Caspar kept watch outside our classroom, I fished inside Caspar's bag. I put Miss Chatto's hairclip in her pen pot on the desk, not clipped on, but down inside it. She wouldn't see it straight away, but she would find it. I put Jake's pen in the box of pencils on top of a pile of portraits.

I put a sticker book, a phone charm and the Eiffel Tower sharpener with the water bottle in the book corner in a plastic pot. I poured all the little things into an empty paint pot and put them on the floor in the book corner. I stood for a moment in the middle of the room listening to the playground sounds.

After that, in the library, we waited until there was nobody about and I pushed *Five O'Clock Charlie* back in a gap in the shelves. Caspar pointed out that it wasn't the right place alphabetically, but I wanted to do it quickly.

I dropped Shabbir's ladybird stone in his pocket in the cloakroom.

When everyone came in for the afternoon, I waited for people to find the things, and it was hard not to look across at Caspar. Theo found the pot in the reading corner and called out, "Hey, these are all the missing things everyone was looking for," and he handed them out to their owners. There was a buzz around the room. People said, "How did they all get there?"

"Maybe the cleaners found them," someone suggested.

Miss Chatto held up her hairclip. "How odd. Look, guys, it's back!" She sounded really excited. "Well, I have no idea how I lost it, but it's strange how much I've missed it. When you lose something, you realise too late what it meant to you." She flexed the gripper. "If you'd never lost it, I suppose you'd never know."

I had been all right up till then but now, suddenly, I thought I might cry. She could've been talking about our house, about my family. Her words were going round and round in my head. *When you lose something, you realise too late what it meant to you. If you'd never lost it, I suppose you'd never know.*

I gulped. I peeped around at all the chatting people in my class. I went still inside myself. *Don't cry. You'll give yourself away. In a minute we'll be doing maths. Think about that.*

Later on Jake appeared back in our class. After a few minutes he held up his fountain pen. "Look what appeared. I'm so pleased to see this. I haven't felt right without it." He turned his back and sketched a monkey on a swing on the flipchart. We all tried to copy the monkey.

I looked over at Caspar. He did the tiniest squeeze together of his lips and a nod.

That evening I'd been invited to Amelia's after school. "Oh, hi," she said, "You can watch me practise my ballet. Come up."

In her bedroom I said I needed the loo and, once

I got in there, I took off the sun top, which I was wearing under my shirt, and hung it on a hook on the back of the door where there was already an old dressing gown. I put my shirt and jumper on again, came back down the corridor and stood in the doorway of her room.

Amelia was in a headstand. "When you have your new house, will you be able to choose what colour your bedroom is?" she asked.

"Maybe," I said.

"You're so lucky," Amelia said. "I decided I hate pink and Mum says I just have to live with it." Amelia looked funny upside down. Her face was very red. "I'm going to stick wrapping paper on the walls until she changes her mind," she said, her legs collapsing.

Amelia thought I was lucky. She was wrong about that, but I did laugh and try to do a handstand too while she held my legs.

We lay on the floor. "Let's watch TV," she said. "I'll ask Mum if we can have popcorn."

I had never explained to Amelia about our house. She didn't know about us maybe losing it or about Mum and Dad drowning in worries and paperwork. And because she didn't know, I could pretend sometimes that I didn't know either.

I wondered who would be first in the bathroom in her family and who would find the sun top and I pictured it being stuffed back inside that huge wardrobe with all the other clothes Amelia hardly ever wore.

Chapter 44
Caspar

We walked to the charity shop together. We had decided what to say and practised, but just before we pushed the door, Ren said, "I can't!"

My heart sank. "Why?"

She was shaking. Turning away. "I don't know. It's too scary."

I made my arms wide and stepped into her path to block her. "It will be fine. Just say what you practised."

"I can't remember it."

"Yes you can."

Ren's eyes were wide with horror. "The woman

in there. She'll recognise me."

"She won't."

We stood outside the shop, blocking the doorway, as if we were glued to the pavement.

"I'm going back to Gran's," she murmured.

"No," I said. "You're not. I'll speak. The least you can do is to stand beside me. It wasn't even me that took it." I was cross now. "Charity shops help people, Ren. Come on!" I grabbed her arm and she let me. *Ding* went the bell over the door. We marched in with me holding Ren's arm like a prisoner.

A lady in a pink jumper was putting price tags on things. She looked up.

Ren shook free from my grip and darted away behind a rack of clothes.

"Hello," I said, carrying on to the till. "Isn't it a nice day? Really mild weather for the time of year."

The woman looked up at me. "Hello," she said.

"Hello," I said again. I beckoned Ren over. "I need you here."

I smiled at the woman. "The thing is, we'd like to make a donation."

Ren appeared beside me now. Her eyes were

wide like a scared mouse. She held a shirt on a hanger in front of her face.

The shop lady frowned and looked from me to Ren and back again.

"Put that down," I murmured.

Ren hooked the shirt on to a rack but then covered her face with her arm instead, as if her fingers had got tangled up by her ear.

"A donation." The woman pushed her glasses up her nose and picked up a notebook and a pen. "That's nice. Did you raise some money with your school?"

"No," we both said.

The woman frowned.

I nudged Ren. She held out her other hand, turned it over, opening the fingers so the money all fell out and coins rolled across the counter. The lady rounded them up and scooped them into her hand.

"This is very kind," she said. "Is this your … sister?"

"No," I said.

Ren looked like a wild hunted creature. She shook her head violently.

"Well … anyway, this is very kind," the woman

said again, staring at Ren.

"It isn't kind," Ren said.

"Oh," said the lady, then: "You're sure you wouldn't like to choose yourselves something? We've got a basket..." She waved towards the kids' stuff at the back of the shop.

"No, thank you," I said, smiling. "Definitely not."

We turned to go but her voice came back. "Do you want me to write down who the donation is from?"

"No," I said. "That wouldn't be a good idea. Goodbye."

Chapter 45
Caspar

We walked back in silence. I felt as if I'd hurt Ren. I knew she had to give the things back but going in the shop seemed to have made her sadder. We found a cat on a wall. It jumped up to be stroked.

"I think it's like a cut healing," I told Ren. "You go on feeling sore. You just will. You will feel better. It's just slow."

"Do you think the woman in the shop recognised me?" Ren asked. "Do you think she was suspicious?"

The cat began making that chirrup noise, twisting and weaving against Ren's fingers.

"Was she the one on the till when you took the bear?"

"Yes."

"I don't know," I said. "She didn't react; not in a dramatic way. She didn't say 'Get out!'"

Ren looked horrified. "I hadn't thought of that," she said. "Imagine if she had. Imagine if she'd shouted 'Get out!' in front of all the customers!"

"But she didn't, which has to be a good thing." I carried on throwing ideas out. "If she did recognise you, she was probably pleased you came and gave her the money."

"But she would still think I'm a bad person," Ren said.

That was tricky. Probably the woman would think that. I mean, most of the world would think that! Ren was looking so worried.

I said, "Well, taking the bear from her shop was bad. It's wrong."

Ren's face was awful now, but I ploughed on. "But the thing is she doesn't know you, does she? And now you've given her the money it's like you're ... putting it right."

"It still feels ... like I'm bad." Ren let the cat nuzzle her fingers.

That must be horrible. That must really hurt to think that someone would just mostly think you're bad. Like that would be their first thought about you.

"I'll never go in there again," Ren said.

I stroked the cat from one end to the other. Its fur had gone electric. I love how a cat's fur does that. "That woman must see a lot of people in a day. She's probably a bit bored," I said.

Ren looked up at me.

"My brother Matty did work experience in that shop and he said some people just come in for a chat and never buy a single thing for weeks and weeks."

"Oh," Ren said. She sighed.

"Anyway, next time you could go in disguise," I said.

Ren chuckled.

"You could borrow a dog."

"You're not allowed dogs in there."

"The thing is, you're making everything better by putting things back. You're making up for it. That's why you'll feel better, when all the things have gone back."

"There's only my gran's bird left now."

"Will you sneak in while she's asleep? That's the kind of thing they do in films."

"No. She might hear me creep in and think I'm a burglar and hit me over the head."

"Don't do that then! Hey, Ren, maybe I could send in the remote-controlled jeep with the bird strapped on top."

"That is ridiculous!" Ren was really laughing now. "It would get stuck in the rug. She's got a really hairy rug right by the bed. And anyway, your jeep would be too noisy."

We went quiet.

"But you do have to put the bird back," I said. "It's like when Snaffle's been leaping in mud again and we have to get him clean. You have to get all the horrible feelings off. Then the good luck will come flooding back."

Chapter 46
Ren

I waited until evening. I checked Gran's bedroom door but, as expected, it was locked.

Petie fell asleep quickly. I kept myself awake. I listened for sounds in the corridor.

I padded down and checked the door again. Still locked.

I would have to wait until she went to bed.

I was sweating and my head pounded. I wouldn't go in when she was actually in the bed, would I?

Yes, I would. I'd promised Caspar. I wished he was with me. The bird felt scratchy in my hand.

I drowsed and lay and sweated.

Sometime later I heard movement going past my room and down the corridor. I leapt out of bed, rushed to the door and peeped out. There it was; her shape disappearing into the bathroom. She must be going to clean her teeth. She told us to do ours for two minutes. Two minutes, that was no time!

Don't mess it up, don't mess it up.

Click … *swish*… I heard the bathroom door closing.

I was as swift as a deer. Down the corridor and in. The night light was on by her bed. I rushed across the floor but, argh, my foot caught on the sheepskin rug. *Thwack.* I hit the side of the bed and rolled, hitting the chest of drawers.

I sprawled.

Oh no … the two minutes. How loud had I been? *Oh no, oh no*… I struggled to get up. *Ow, ow!*

I heard Gran's voice. "Who's there? Is someone there?"

A terrible figure in the open doorway, weird green face, hair in an odd band, white nightie and dressing gown. I gasped. Gran but so different. Like … a Halloween character.

"Ren? What are you doing in my room?" Her

usual sharp voice.

That weird green face. The pain in my foot…

Something snapped in me. "I … I…" I picked up the bird from the floor. She was coming towards me. "Where did you get *that*?" Her voice was full of hardness. "There's no use lying to me, Ren."

My legs buckled. I thought about curling up on the rug. I looked up into her craggy ghost face and I couldn't think of anything clever to say. "I took it."

She blinked.

"Why?" Her voice was low and wobbly now. "Why did you take it?"

"I don't know," I said in a really small voice. My head was full of nothing. "I don't know." Tears came in my eyes. "I just … did it and now I wanted to give it back."

"You were putting the bird *back*?"

"Yes."

"Oh, Ren." Gran looked at me as if she'd never met me. Maybe now she would throw us out. Tell Mum and Dad. They would be so ashamed of me.

"I would've. I know where it goes. I came in … but I tripped over the rug!"

Gran's face staring at me was pale green with dark eye pits. She was like a ghoul coming for me.

I squeezed my eyes shut. "Please don't tell Mum and Dad. They're drowning with worries about the money and losing the house and the contract. They're full up!"

She wouldn't understand. She would kick us out and we'd be back in the B&B with the rat. Maybe she would tell school about a girl she knew who stole things in the house where she had been allowed to stay. That bad one. I put my head in my hands.

She lowered herself on to the rug beside me. "That's a lot of worries. No wonder you've been looking miserable."

I peeped round. Her face was really terrible – like green lava. I shut my eyes again. "Tell me," she said gently.

In the gold glow from the night light I told Gran about the *My Life in a Box* project at school. Except not Gran, the ghost Gran. I told her about not having anything for the box and finding I was clever at stealing. She sat still, close beside me. Soon I was telling her how I took Amelia's sun top and

Jake's pen and all the other things. I was gulping and reaching the end. "Caspar is helping me put everything back," I told her. "I never really wanted the things."

"Well," she said when the room went silent. "Well…"

I braced myself. But then I felt her hand on my shoulder. "Ren." Her hand pressed. And then her voice came closer. "Ren, I think you've been in … rather a dark place, am I right?"

I nodded.

"You've been coping with such a lot. I hadn't appreciated … not really… You and I haven't had a good start, have we? I've lived on my own for years. It really is very hard to have a whole family move in and I have tried … to make things nice."

I felt bad. I thought about the screaming and the running.

Gran put her fingers on the sides of her forehead and pressed there. "I do actually get headaches," she said.

"I thought you just meant that we were a headache; Petie and me, like … annoying."

She shook her head. "I don't like a fuss. I'm so sorry you've felt so alone. I don't imagine you felt you could talk to me about all of this either. I'm not the most… I mean, I was brought up to do practical things, but I don't always know what to say." She sighed. "And you have to understand, this is my home. I am trying to help, but sometimes it seems as if you don't like me very much."

"I'm sorry about the screaming and the smashing and the mess…"

"Those are not the most important things. Not in the end." She moved closer beside me on the floor.

"I … I … just miss our house," I said.

Her arm came round me. "It's going to be OK," she said. Her dressing gown was very soft. My head was lost in the warm softness of it.

Now I cried for everything we'd lost: our normal life, our house in the street I knew, my bedroom with all the little things I'd saved and made, the rainbows and the clouds, all our family world. I cried until I was empty.

Gran held me close. "I think you have had to be very grown-up very suddenly," she said. "You've helped your brother cope. I know he's been infuriating but … that's what brothers are for."

I thought of all the Mr Softie stories I'd made up and the terrible night when Petie had set off to try to find him. Petie was in his bed now in the brown spare room, curled up and warm.

"You've done your best," Gran said.

I felt around on the floor and found the real-feather bird with the twig legs. I handed it to Gran.

"Scratchy little thing." She held it up to her face. She did a little cough. "To be honest … well, I'm not actually sure I was supposed to own this. It was my aunt's. I remember wanting it. I don't think she ever actually said I could have it."

I stared at Gran's strange craggy green face. Something dropped away inside me.

"I rather like little objects … ornaments. Look." She got up. "Come and see." She led me to the small cupboard with the glass doors. "They're things from holidays mostly. I love anything made from glass."

I gazed in at the sparkly things on the shelves, glass fish with flicking tails, a blue dolphin, a box covered in tiny stones.

Gran gently put the bird back inside and closed the cupboard doors. "Would you like to have a proper look tomorrow?"

"Yes."

She sighed. "It's very late. Shall we say

goodnight?" Some of the green splodgy stuff had dripped down in little rivers from her eyes. I realised she must have cried too.

"You look like a ghost, Gran," I said.

"Face pack," she said, smiling until it cracked.

Chapter 47
Caspar

I found Jake on Monday in the corridor outside the classroom.

We looked around us.

"Well?" he said.

"It's done," I said. I felt a bit like a spy talking in code.

"All gone back?"

I nodded. "Everything."

"Good man," he said.

We melted away by the door.

Chapter 48
Ren

We were upstairs in the brown spare room. I was lying on my bed reading. Petie was on the floor playing.

Dad called from downstairs. "Foood!"

He used to call like that in the old days, but nobody shouted to people like that at Gran's.

Petie put down the animal he was talking to. "Dad shouted."

"I know."

"Where's Gran?"

Something different was in the air when we arrived in the kitchen. Mum was humming, actually humming. She was pouring fizzy drinks.

"Pizza's cooking," Dad said.

Petie and me looked at each other. We both mouthed, "*PIZZA?*"

"Then we're going to watch a film," Mum said.

"Is it someone's birthday?" Petie said, plonking himself down on a chair.

"Nope," Dad said.

We gathered round the table and the pizza came out of the oven all hot and steaming with delicious toppings. Dad began cutting it.

"Where's Gran gone?" Petie asked.

"She's visiting a friend," Dad said. "And it's a chance to be … just us."

"Should we still get the napkins out?" I asked.

"No. No napkins," Dad said.

"We thought we might do this on Saturdays every week. Just be us," Mum said. We all had slices of pizza now.

"Can we eat the pizza with our hands?" I asked.

"Gran doesn't like it, but she isn't here," Petie added.

"Go for it," Mum said.

We ate pizza and slurped our drinks, all the time

watching Mum and Dad. They looked different. It was as if there was more air in the room.

When the food was finished, Dad cleared the plates and Mum said, "Well..." She looked at Dad. "We do have some good news. The insurance people have agreed on the house."

"Does that mean we can go home?" Petie said.

"There isn't a house yet," I said. "It's not like ... magic."

"It's OK, love. It means our house can be rebuilt, Petie," Dad said.

Mum chipped in. "It might look different from how it used to when it's finished. We'll have to think about it and talk to builders. But the main thing is, it's agreed. And that's brilliant."

They hugged us.

"But it will still take a long time. Months. They would pay for us to live in a different house until ours is ready," Mum said.

"So not at Gran's?" I asked.

"We'll have a chat with her," Dad said. "We're OK staying here at the moment, I think. We'll definitely be here for Christmas."

"What will Father Christmas do?" Petie asked.

"He'll come here, to Gran's," Mum said.

"Shall I leave him a note?"

Mum smiled. "That's a good idea. We'll go to our old house and leave him a note."

Chapter 49
Ren

Gran started to let us watch TV and pin things on the walls in the brown spare room. Caspar often came for tea and we sometimes went for a walk with him and Snaffle.

I didn't steal any more. When I thought about it, I always pictured Caspar's face the first time he found the Shadowbox and how upset he'd been.

I still felt empty sometimes. I still dreamed of the fire and imagined hanging off my bedroom as the flames rose around me, but those were just dreams.

Chapter 50
Ren

By now it was the end of November. Next week was the exhibition in the school hall with all our class's work on display. I still didn't have much ready except my wild self-portrait, Gran's photos of me and Petie, one feeding a horse and some old family birthday ones. I also had the copies of some paintings I did in school, but pictures seemed like the wrong things for a box.

We walked around town with Gran on Saturday afternoon and Christmas cards were on sale at a stall by the church. Gran suddenly said, "You both wait for me here," and she came back with advent calendars for each of us with chocolates inside. The rule was that from the first of December we could open a numbered window each day and eat one.

When we got home, I sat staring at my advent calendar. The sparkly picture had glitter sprinkled on to look like snow. It showed a wood filled with animals with a huge tree in the middle. Every window in the advent calendar had an animal peeping out from a tree or a hole in the ground. An idea came to me.

I ran downstairs. "Gran," I said, "do you have some cardboard, glue and scissors?"

"Yes," she said. "Let's clear the table."

Gran helped me find stuff. I tipped out the art materials I'd been given after the fire. I found a notebook and wrote a list. I had to practise drawing all the people and each thing small enough to fit.

I very gently prised open one window of my calendar, not for the chocolate; just to understand how it worked. Then I propped it up so I could look at it while I made my own version.

I laid two pieces of card one on top of the other and marked out my own small squares with a fold down the side so each one could be opened. It was fiddly. I took my time. Next I got out the pencils and paints and began my picture.

I worked all weekend on my artwork and it was ready to carry into school on Monday for the exhibition.

I called it "Ren's Dream House". It was a picture of a house, but not a real house – it was a normal house shape but bigger with loads of windows, a roof with sloping sides and a flat top. My house had a big garden with a fence along the front and flowers and birds in the tree. I had carefully added details like window boxes and chimneys. And above the house I had painted the blue sky with a few clouds and more than one rainbow.

I knew it was my best drawing. I found Jake as soon as I got to school and explained that my work would need to go on the wall. "I think your artwork is terrific," he said, helping me put it up.

Parents began to arrive. On all the tables around the hall were the boxes with all the objects labelled and explained and up on the wall was my Dream House.

People loved being able to open and close the windows. Inside each one, I had put a person waving: Mum and Dad, Gran, Petie with Mr

Softie, Amelia. Jake, Miss Chatto and Mr Charles were in there and other people from my class like Theo, Shabbir and Ellie.

Caspar stood with Snaffle on the front doorstep.

I was waving from my own room in the house. Around me were things that had been in my collections; crowding along the windowsill were glass animals, souvenirs and models.

Mine was the only artwork on the wall, but Shabbir had his stones on display and quite a few people had things out on the tables that were too big for their boxes.

In his speech Jake said, "I love all the ways these children have shown us what makes them who they are. Each one is so different. They are just brilliant."

Chapter 51
Caspar

On the exhibition day Mum and Dad came into school with the other parents to see what we'd all done. I saw Matty's face grinning out at me from Dad's phone. "Sorry I can't be there," he said. "I thought you could give me a tour."

"Oh, wow, yes," I said. I carried the phone around and showed him all the artworks, like a tour guide. "That's clever," he said when I showed him Shabbir's stones. "Nearer. I need to see them properly."

"Here's the artist," I said, close-upping on Shabbir.

Shabbir bowed.

Matty thought Ren's advent house idea was amazing. "I would never have thought of this in a million years," I told him.

I showed him the contents of my box. "Is that the instructions for the jeep?" he said.

"Yeah, well, the jeep was too big to fit," I said.

There were lots of photos of Snaffle along with one of his chew toys, a book I used to read and some poems about moths. I did have a model of a space capsule used in the lunar landings, but Snaffle had chewed it. I wrote about expeditions to the Arctic because I've always liked reading about expeditions.

"It's great," Matty said. "Thanks for showing me round."

It was good that Matty came, that he wanted to. He was the only virtual visitor to the exhibition.

The teachers said well done to Ren, but they should really have said more. She should have talked to our whole class and taught all of us to make advent calendars. It was an excellent idea. But I don't think Ren wanted to do that.

You can't really put someone's life in a box. But the boxes did look amazing in the school hall. Miss Chatto cried and hugged some of the parents. Mum and Dad chatted to Ren's parents and her gran.

A few days later Ren took me to see her actual house that had burned down. We walked round after school.

They're going to start rebuilding it soon. It's more of a gap than a house at the moment. I didn't say that to Ren obviously. I said, "Let's come back every month and take a picture – then you'll be able to see how it's changing."

She nodded. "OK."

I asked the builders some questions. One day, I think my brother Matty might design houses and build them. That's what his degree is for. I had told him on the phone about Ren's house. "Must've been a bad fire," he said.

When he's back at Christmas, maybe he could come with us to see Ren's house – by then the builders will be laying the foundations.

I'm still getting the bus with Dad, Ren and Petie in the mornings and going round to Ren's gran's after school.

Ren and Petie are my friends now, like, properly.

I think Ren's gran is a prickly person but she's

all right. She can be really funny. You just have to watch her to check she thinks something's funny too before you laugh.

Last time I went round there for tea, she pulled me to one side when I was laying the table and said, "You have done so much good, you know, Caspar."

We had a moment of staring at each other, and I wondered if Ren had told her about the stealing or whether maybe she guessed. She won't tell anyone, though. I mean, if she's been a head teacher, she's probably kept loads of secrets.

I said, "You've done lots of good for this family too."

"Oh, Caspar," she said, shaking her head. "Oh, Caspar."

I didn't know what to say, and she seemed to be waiting, so I said, "I actually think your cooking is better than my mum and dad's." I'm sure she won't tell them. Mum and Dad don't really enjoy cooking; they just heat things up when they have to. I am the one who enjoys it.

And I had another thought. "Do you think you could teach me and Ren how to make lasagne? I've always wanted to make lasagne and when I had it for tea here I thought it was remarkable!"

Ren's gran smiled. "I would love to do that, Caspar," she said.

Chapter 52
Ren

At Christmas Petie gave me a present. He was hopping around, all excited as I unwrapped it. "There was a book sale," he said. "In school. They were selling old library books that nobody borrowed. I saw this. Dad helped me buy it." He grinned across at Dad. "Open it!"

I pulled off the paper. In my hands was *Five O'Clock Charlie*, the book we had lost in the fire, the book I had stolen and then given back to the library. Now it was mine. Properly mine. I turned it over and over. There was the horse gazing over the fence with his big sad eyes. I flicked through it and stroked the cover. My little brother kept jumping up and down like a crazy excited bug.

"Thank you," I said, reaching out to hug him. "It's my favourite book."

"I knew that!" he chimed.

I could put *Five O'Clock Charlie* out on a shelf, leave it there and read it whenever I wanted. I didn't have to hide it.

It's going to be months before our house is ready to move back into. I don't know how long we will go on staying in the brown spare room at Gran's, but I have some things in the bedside cupboard now and a desk where I can do my homework. For Christmas Gran got me a little glass-doored cupboard to start my own collection of little things.

And then there was a surprise: as we all sat eating dinner a few days ago, Gran said to Dad, "Why don't you carry on staying here until the house is ready? I think we're all getting used to each other."

And I think she's right: we are.

Maybe I was wrong when I thought I had lost everything in our house fire. I think I lost the real me for a while. But now I think she's coming back.

Chapter 53
Ren

Last weekend, Petie had gone to a friend's house and Caspar and me took Snaffle for a walk. It was cold but sunny and we ran and chased him around the trees in the park. Snaffle actually behaved quite well and only barked at one cyclist. Afterwards we sat on the bench in Gran's garden where Snaffle was allowed now as long as he was on his lead, and Caspar showed me how to train Snaffle to lie down by pointing a finger and going, "*Lie down*," in a forceful way "No treat unless he does it," Caspar said. "You have to not give in."

I stroked Snaffle's silky ears. Something was on

my mind. "I've been thinking... In your house, where do you keep the dog treats?"

"Well, we haven't really got a container for them. Snaffle does have his own cupboard," Caspar said. "We just pile the new packets on the shelf."

"Just a minute." I got up and went up the garden and into the house. I collected the thing I needed and carried it back outside.

Caspar's mouth opened wide. Tight against my chest, I was holding my Shadowbox...

"I want you to have this, Caspar, for Snaffle's treats," I told him. "I think it would ... work better in your house." I ran my fingers over the dark charcoal top with its dents and the ghostly circus picture. "Now I can think of this having a home in your kitchen. And I can buy extra treats and bring them round sometimes."

"That's a great idea," Caspar said. "The tin will keep filling up and there will never be space in it for ... anything else."

"The lid doesn't really fit?" I said, pressing round the warped edge.

"Don't worry," he said. "I might be able to hammer it back into shape. And he gets through the packets of treats quite fast."

I put the tin into his arms. “I just … like thinking of it going to Snaffle,” I said.

“It’s a brilliant idea,” Caspar said. “Your tin will always be full.”

“Thank you.” I smiled then. “I mean it, Caspar … thank you.”

Acknowledgements

Many writers and friends told me accounts of childhood misdemeanours to help me shape this book and explore Ren's state of mind. Thank you to everyone who spoke to me from their hearts on the theme of stealing.

Big thanks in particular to:

My writers' group (Julian, Kryss, Alison, Lesley and Yvonne), who always offer such great ideas and feedback.

Anna Bright for telling me about family memories and about Mr Softie.

Barbara Lafon for her psychological insights.

Sue Wallman, Jess Palmer, Sue Durrant and Ulla Kingsley for insights and suggestions.

My editor Kirsty Stansfield and the whole amazing team at Nosy Crow.

My agent Anne Clark, whose wisdom and advice are always spot on.

Tom Bonnick, who was my sounding board for early ideas.

And, of course, my fantastic family, the Howes and the Briggses, who always support me so well.

We all need a Caspar in our lives. Although I will never be able to thank them personally, the children Caspar is based on will always have a special place in my thoughts.